His lips came down hot and hard in a scorching kiss.

She made a futile attempt to push him off, but it was like a kitten fighting a tiger. He easily overpowered her and held her for a long embrace that, strangely, began with a ruthless attack and eased to gentleness as Esther stopped struggling. When he released her, she gazed mutely at his darkly dilated eyes. He looked rather startled, and so did she.

"You'll be giving me ideas you're the kissing bandit," she said.

"I knew what you were thinking. Since I was suspected of such villany, I foolishly decided to play the part. It was rash. I do apologize."

Also by Joan Smith
Published by Fawcett Books:

BABE
AURORA
IMPRUDENT LADY
LACE OF MILADY
VALERIE
THE BLUE DIAMOND
REPRISE
WILES OF A STRANGER
LOVER'S VOWS
RELUCTANT BRIDE
LADY MADELINE'S FOLLY
LOVE BADE ME WELCOME
MIDNIGHT MASQUERADE
ROYAL REVELS
THE DEVIOUS DUCHESS
TRUE LADY
BATH BELLES
STRANGE CAPERS
A COUNTRY WOOING
LOVE'S HARBINGER
LETTERS TO A LADY
COUNTRY FLIRT
LARCENOUS LADY
MEMOIRS OF A HOYDEN
SILKEN SECRETS
DRURY LANE DARLING
THE HERMIT'S DAUGHTER

THE ROYAL SCAMP

Joan Smith

FAWCETT CREST • NEW YORK

A Fawcett Crest Book
Published by Ballantine Books
Copyright © 1989 by Joan Smith

Library of Congress Catalog Card Number: 88-92910

ISBN 0-449-21610-1

Manufactured in the United States of America

First Edition: May 1989

Chapter One

Esther Lowden sat alone that evening in her small but elegant Rose Saloon, comparing the merits of a pink sprigged muslin versus a jonquil striped afternoon gown, when the butler announced, "Mr. Ramsay, Miss Lowden."

"Oh, good. Show him in," she said, thinking it was Joshua Ramsay's cousin Buck, her manager, come to make his evening report.

Her face fell when it was Joshua who strode in, wearing a scowl that masqueraded as a smile. "Not serving ale in the tavern this evening, Esther?" he asked, the smile dwindling to a sneer.

"Nice to see you, too, Joshua," she answered in the same thin tone. "Have a seat—or is this one of your fleeting calls, to complain of noise and dust from the Lowden Arms?"

"Not this time. In fact, your inn is very nearly deserted. You will be regretting you destroyed a perfectly good mansion by turning it into a public house. I counted two carriages in the yard as I drove past."

"My customers have the bizarre habit of keeping their carriages and cattle in the stable, not standing outdoors. I happen to know I had an even dozen rooms let at four o'clock this afternoon. I expect by dark there were as many again. Travelers will usually pelt along till the shadows lengthen, you know."

"You dined there, did you?"

"No, Buck dined here, and told me."

"I hope you had a chaperon with you," he said swiftly, looking around to see if her aunt was hiding behind a chair or under a table.

"My aunt dined with us, thus depriving your cousin of an excellent opportunity to molest me. Tell me, is it seduction you have in mind as well? Shall I call the butler and request him to bring a pistol?"

"Already the coarsening influence of your profession is beginning to tell. Two years ago you would not have used such language with a gentleman."

"Two years ago no gentleman was in the delightful habit of reading me a lecture every time we met. You used to be more amusing, Joshua. Sit down, for goodness' sake. Why must you lounge against a table like a lazy servant instead of using the posture of a gentleman," she said sharply.

Ramsay removed his elbow from the high table and strolled farther into the room, looking with distaste at the chamber. "Do you not feel like a bird in a cage in this box?" he asked.

"The saloon is twenty feet by thirty. It is sufficiently large for me. If *you* are feeling constrained, however . . ."

He lifted one black brow in disdain. "You ought not to greet gentlemen without a chaperon, Esther. It is unusual in the extreme for a young lady to do so. And as far as Lady Brown goes, I'm not at all sure that aged and flighty woman is sufficient protection," he informed her.

"After rooting about in the dusty corners of your

mind, is 'aged and flighty' the best insult you can come up with? It is an old English custom for widows to be flighty. You must lay the blame for my being unattended, as for all other little lapses, on my having opened Lowden Hall up to travelers," she told him.

He gazed at her a long moment, shaking his head ruefully. "No, you were unusual even before that. You were always a harum-scarum girl—running hot after you knew not what."

"But I *do* know what, Joshua. That is what you refuse to understand. I want more from life than to vegetate in the country. I want to see a face other than family or neighbor from time to time. I did not sell Lowden Hall and go abroad as I wanted to when Papa died, so you need not ring a peal over me for what I did. It was you who suggested I find an absorbing hobby."

"I meant embroidery or watercolors!" Her scathing look told him her opinion of these occupations. "It would almost be better if you had gone abroad for a spell. That might have settled you down, and there would not be the sort of shadow attached to it that attaches to a well-born lady turning publican."

"Ah, but who would you pharisees have to turn your noses down at, if it were not for us publicans?" she chided. "Not that I am, strictly speaking, a publican. I don't even own the Lowden Arms."

"You are playing with words."

"No, no! Ideas. You should try it sometime, Joshua. I am the major partner in the Lowden Investment Company. My aunt is a minor partner. The company happens to own and operate an inn, among its other assets."

"Its other asset being this dower house you re-side in, when you're not trotting about the inn like a common—" She stopped him with a bright, gimlet eye.

"We own various properties," she said airily. "Real estate, I suppose is the branch of business we are in, Auntie and I." Of course Joshua knew that the only properties owned were the two mentioned.

"When a person feels obliged to hide her calling, you may take it for granted she is, in fact, ashamed of it. You own and operate an inn, and it is beneath a lady of quality to do so."

Esther's shoulders twitched in impatience. "Too much is beneath a lady of quality. If all we may, with propriety, do is sit on our thumbs waiting for some jackanapes to marry us, then I resign from the quality. Tell me, is your cousin Buck also cast into the outer darkness for aiding and abetting me? He is an excellent manager."

"How you ever talked Buck into this piece of folly is beyond my comprehension," he charged.

"But then, so much is beyond your comprehension, is it not?" she asked, and smiled demurely.

He looked at her aslant, frustration burning at his vitals. Why had he come here? He knew Esther was impossible. To add to his chagrin, she had succeeded in casting *him* in the role of outdated ogre ranting at her success. "There is also a good deal beyond yours, Esther. I shouldn't think, at three and twenty, you have entirely given up hope of nabbing a husband. Don't expect any gentleman of character to offer marriage to a woman who runs a common inn."

She heard that demeaning "woman" in lieu of "lady" and reined in her temper. "We feel, Buck and I, that the Lowden Arms is something quite out of the common. It is top of the trees, I promise you.

4

We had two lords and a knight staying there last week. Lord Eskett told me personally it was the finest establishment of its kind within fifty miles of London."

"He happened to mention it as you served his mutton?" he asked with a mocking smile.

"No, I encountered Lord and Lady Eskett while strolling along the Thames, in the delightful private garden the Lowden Arms provides its guests. The countess and I agreed the place is charming. They sang its praises so loud I was a little embarrassed to come out and say I owned it—indirectly, through the Lowden Investment Company, of course," she added hastily.

"They would not have been speaking to you in a social way had they realized your calling."

"You say my 'calling' as though I were a hangman! I can only assume that my character is not so grossly coarsened as you have been telling me. They did not take me for a publican to talk to me but for a lady."

"Word of it is bound to leak out eventually. Once such persons as Eskett realize what you are up to, they may continue to patronize the Arms, but they will not expect to speak to you as an equal, nor to speak to you at all, except in the way of business."

Esther twitched her shoulders. "That will be a great loss to me; I always had so much to do with fine lords and ladies!"

"You could have had. You should have gone to London and made your debut instead of this freakish start. . . ."

She turned a fiery eye on him. "You are overlooking a few points, Joshua. A lady does not go up to London with an empty purse. I opened my house to guests to make a living. The estate was so mortgaged when Father died, I had to sell off all the land. How was I to go on living in a mansion on nothing a year? Tell me that, wizard!"

"And you didn't even tell me it was for sale! You *knew* I wanted to enlarge the Abbey. Our lands ran together."

"What did you plan to use for money? You were complaining at the time that your own father left you land rich, cash poor. You never indicated any interest in buying. I am not a mind reader after all."

"If selling was your only recourse, you might better have sold the whole thing—lock, stock, and barrel—and lived on the income of your capital, like a lady."

"That, unfortunately, would not have provided a ladylike existence."

"It would have provided better than this," he said, sweeping a condemning arm around the saloon.

"This is only temporary. I made three thousand profit my first year of operation. How many thousand pounds must I have had to make that sort of income?" His eyes widened in surprise, and she rushed on to push her advantage. "Why, in five years or so I shall be so rich, the royal dukes themselves will be offering for my hand."

"The royal dukes may," he agreed with a malicious twinkle in his eyes, "but no gentleman of taste and refinement will."

"Good, that will save me the bother of refusing them. I don't know why men think we must be forever on the catch for a husband. I am perfectly happy as I am."

"Till the novelty wears off," he countered.

"There is always another novelty. That's half the

charm of it. A constant stream of strangers, bringing variety to life."

He stared blankly. "What pleasure can you *possibly* find in entertaining strangers?"

"Why, Joshua, you astonish me! You have your own book in the Bible, and you don't know we are enjoined 'to entertain strangers'!"

"A hazardous business. You might be entertaining cutthroats or thieves."

"Or 'angels unawares.' But then, you are a confirmed pessimist, and I shan't confuse you with any cheerful thoughts. Have you read any good obituaries lately?" she asked, and picked up the journal.

Always alive to a hint, Joshua immediately got to his feet. "I see you have better things to do than entertain a mere friend. A pity I hadn't the advantage of being completely unknown, and you and I might—" He stopped short, and while he didn't blush or stammer, there was a self-conscious air about him.

While he stood looking at Esther, she puzzled this half remark. It was possible to read into it a hint he had come courting. If so, it was a new wrinkle in their relationship. They had discussed nothing but her "calling" ever since she opened the inn. He used to be more conciliating before her father's death. Still, she had been a full one and twenty at the time, and he had never come up to scratch.

And she was glad, for she didn't know then, and still didn't know, whether she would accept him. Ramsay was considered the prime parti in the neighborhood. He was the owner of Heath Abbey, a huge, sprawling estate stolen from the monks by Henry VIII eons ago and given to one of Ramsay's ancestors for some chicanery they were involved in together.

In the gallery of Heath Abbey there were portraits of the family going back to the fifteenth century. The pirates who had preceded that time were not so prominently displayed. The males had changed remarkably little over the years. With an older hairstyle and jacket, Joshua might be taken in a dim light for his first painted ancestor. They all had black hair, ruler straight, a pronounced point in the middle of the forehead, dark eyes, a predatory beak of a nose, and a jaw that might have been formed from a set square. From the scowls hanging on the wall, it seemed they had always been sharp tempered as well.

Esther felt she would be very out of place amid the females of the line. The Ramsay gentlemen preferred grenadiers of women, or had so little choice in the matter that they married gigantic antidotes in any case. If you stuck a mustache or beard on any one of the ladies, she might pass for a man, and not a weak man, either. Joshua's own mama had been not far from six feet in height, with a pair of shoulders that would turn a dragoon green with envy. And with her physique she had the disposition of a little mouse.

Esther, though slight in frame, was not at all biddable. She had inherited her mother's auburn hair and brown eyes and, unfortunately, her tendency to turn brown as a nut in the sun. From her father she got a certain wilfulness that did not take kindly to advice, especially from outsiders. Her streak of practicality was not inherited from either parent, but sprang up like a mushroom when she was faced with a crisis after her papa's death and led to her "calling."

Lowden Arms, née Lowden Hall, seat of the Lowdens of Berkshire for the past three hundred years or so, was one of the ugliest heaps of stones ever piled one on top of the other. It had no grace, no charm, but was a tall brownstone building with a pair of angle turrets guarding either end that added to its fortresslike air. It had a crenellated roofline, with a little domed arch set in the middle of the roof, on which one of her ancestors had erected a metal statue of himself in armor, which had since weathered to a rusty green. The house had twenty-six handsome bedchambers on the first floor and another twenty only slightly less handsome above that. The second-story roof was low, so that the charge for those rooms was less.

Lowden Hall had had impressive double oak doors with the family crest done in concrete work above. The concrete had since been covered in brass with some enameling to bring the arms into prominence. A few other renovations had occurred as well to transform a private residence into a commercial establishment. Joshua Ramsay had had a great deal to say against all these renovations. The words "sacrilege" and "desecration" rang in Esther's ears, as though it were St. Paul's Cathedral she was changing and not an ugly old house.

None of her work so incensed him as the elegant brass plaque, only about fifteen inches square—one would think it was a broadsheet. Engraved on it in the best of good, discreet taste and the finest Gothic script were the simple words Lowden Arms—Dining and Accommodation. To call it vulgar was ridiculous, and to call it criminal was a plain lie. She had secured her license in the usual way, by a hefty bribe.

The stables had had to be enlarged. Esther confessed to a twinge at seeing the old garden cobbled over for a stable yard. One thing she did not have to desecrate was the wonderful location. The Thames flowed idly by, a few hundred yards behind the Hall, and the willows still wept over it. It was a popular walk for guests on a fine afternoon.

When all her renovations were done, Esther removed to the dower house with her aunt, Lady Brown, to save the disgrace of saying she actually ran the inn herself. Her solicitor gravely informed her that for a lady to have the wits and will to make money was beneath contempt, so he set up the investment company to put her at one remove from commerce. It was a ruse that didn't fool the locals, but if ever she became rich and decided to try the London marriage mart, it would sound respectable.

It happened that Buck Ramsay, Joshua's cousin, had a falling out with his father just prior to the opening and was happy to act as manager. Buck usually came over to the dower house every night to fill Esther in on the details of how her business was progressing. He entered on that evening just as Joshua and she were staring at each other. Buck had escaped the Ramsay looks. He was slighter of frame than his cousin, lighter of complexion, smaller of nose, and altogether a more agreeable specimen, though somewhat dandyish in appearance.

"Your clerk has arrived to hand over the day's receipts," Joshua said with a satirical grin at his cousin.

"My manager has come to make his report," she corrected, and winked at Buck. "I never sully my genteel hands with money. How much did I take in, Buck?"

"Twenty-eight rooms taken," Buck reported. "Not including Lady Gloria Devere." He went to the wine table and poured himself a glass.

To assuage Joshua's temper, Esther offered him wine.

"Is it from your inn?" he inquired.

"Yes."

"Then I'll pass."

"A pity I hadn't known you were coming, and I might have got in some hemlock," Esther snipped. "How is old Lady Gloria, Buck?" Not that she cared, but it was a thorn in Joshua's side that such a noble old relict as Lord Grodon's spinster daughter had taken up permanent residence at the Lowden Arms, bringing a whiff of nobility with her.

"Poorly. She never owns up to good health, though she'll outlive the lot of us. We served sixty dinners, all told," he added. "We'll have to think of buying new china. I've been looking through some catalogs. I think pink would add eye appeal to Peters's dinners."

Joshua stared to hear a man discuss such feminine details.

"It is our excellent location that accounts for the extra meals," Esther explained to him. "Close to Windsor and, of course, Strawberry Hill, where the tourists are always eager to see Mr. Walpole's Gothic monstrosity."

"The location is far from ideal," Joshua said. "Too close to London for folks traveling west from it to be ready for a stop, and too close for those traveling east to draw a halt. With London only a few miles away, they will go ahead rather than put up at an inn."

"Twenty-eight travelers seem to be unaware of it today. Of course London is more than a few miles away. And there is Hounslow Heath to be traversed, where the highwaymen do me a very good turn. Travelers are so frightened of them, they rarely venture past my place unless they can reach London before dark. As our reputation spreads and they know they will find a good meal and a well-aired bed awaiting them, they stop over for dinner and remain the night."

"That's true," Buck agreed. "I personally see that every bed is aired after use. From five o'clock on we have carriages pulling in every ten minutes. All the travelers say the same thing; they might as well call it a day, for they won't tackle Hounslow Heath with dark coming on. The highwaymen are getting bolder by the day. Captain Johnnie is the main culprit."

"I don't know why Bow Street doesn't set up a stronger patrol on the heath," Joshua grumbled.

"He would like to see my business ruined," Esther joked to Buck.

"It would take a downturn if they ever captured Captain Johnnie," Buck said, and refilled his glass. He was not much atuned to a joke.

"Then I hope he runs free for a good many years yet."

Joshua bristled, but whether it was her support of the Royal Scamp or Buck's making free with the wine that caused it, she couldn't say. "Just the foolish attitude I would expect you to take!"

"You know where to place the blame," she told him airily.

"I suppose you're half in love with the rogue, like all the ladies. They were singing a ballad in his honor last week in London. 'The Royal Scamp' it is called. Making a hero of a villain—a common thief."

"You have all the romance of a turnip, Joshua," Esther told him. "How could any lady in her right mind fail to be in love with a dashing highwayman who dares to attack whole caravans single-handed?

They say he is very gentlemanly, too. Why, Mrs. Heskett, who had the pleasure of being robbed by him, said he left her very fine diamond wedding ring on her finger rather than hurt her by pulling it off, for it was a trifle tight, you know. I daresay, all wedding rings bind after a while," she added mischievously.

"If he works alone, he hadn't much choice, had he?" Joshua asked. "If he put down his pistol to yank a tight ring off, it wouldn't be long before the men in the carriage would overcome him."

"That is one explanation for his gallantry. He seems to be safe from attack while he kisses all the ladies, at least. Odd none of the gentlemen bother to overpower him then. One would think that would nudge them out of their cowardice if anything would, to see their women being mauled by a criminal." Before Joshua could think of a setdown, she turned to Buck and inquired about her guests.

Joshua disliked being left out of the discussion, or perhaps it was the subject matter that displeased him. "If we are sunk to discussing housekeeping, I shall run along. Are you coming, Buck?"

"I haven't finished my wine," Buck told him.

"Drink it up. You won't want to remain alone with an unchaperoned lady."

"That is true, Buck," Esther agreed. "You wouldn't want to sink so low as your cousin. The fact that you are alone with me every other night of the week is no excuse to do it now, when Joshua is afraid to go home alone. He fears Captain Johnnie may abandon the heath and go after to him."

"I would be very happy to tangle with the rogue, alone or otherwise," Joshua boasted.

Esther rolled her eyes ceilingward and sighed. "Ah, so would I! Preferably alone."

13

"Come along, Buck," Joshua repeated irritably.

Buck drank up his wine, and they left. Esther sat on alone, mulling over their conversation. Joshua's visits always upset her. She felt it her duty to love him and marry him. Her father had expected it, and Lady Brown still pushed the idea forward. But how could you love a man with no sense of humor? Joshua hadn't used to be so dour. It was her turning her home into an inn that had robbed him of his former spirits.

How could anyone envisage being Mrs. Joshua Ramsay, hanging on the Abbey wall with all those dull grenadiers? No, she couldn't possibly marry him, but if others of his class shared his opinion, then turning Lowden Hall into the Lowden Arms had made her ineligible. That was what bothered her. Twenty-three years old. Her looks, such as they were, wouldn't last forever, and despite her proud boast, she didn't want to grow old living in the dower house with her aunt. She wanted much more from life than that. She sighed, blew out the lamps, and went upstairs to bed.

Chapter Two

There were periods when Esther didn't darken the door of the Lowden Arms from head to toe of the week. Spring was not one of those times. When the fashionable people were on the road traveling to London for the season, going to each other's country homes, or just out enjoying a drive in the country, often stopping for lunch or dinner at her hostelry, she was tempted to slip over and take a meal in her old dining room, which she did not call the common room. The public dining room was so elegant, her paying guests could sit down without fear of rubbing shoulders with undesirables. Her prices ensured keeping such clients at the Black Knight, a few miles down the road.

She had an additional excuse for going to the inn, as she kept the family nags at the inn stable. A footboy could bring Flame to her, but on a fine day in April, with the sun beckoning overhead, with a view of the inn from her bedroom window above the intervening row of stately poplars showing bright gowns and dashing blue jackets, she decided to stroll over to the inn herself and have Flame saddled up. She was always careful to have the escort of a groom to lend her dignity. A canter into the village to visit the modiste was her outing.

Esther went down to breakfast in her riding habit, to see her aunt, Lady Brown, fiddling with her poached eggs. Lady Brown was as elegant as a hundred pounds a year could make her. Her husband—a knight, not a baronet—had left her nearly penniless, but Esther gave her a pension as well as room and board. The chaperon was a plump matron of sixty years, with a round pink face that belied her astringent nature. She looked like one of those jolly old ladies, but she was, in fact, a complainer.

"I hear Joshua Ramsay dropped in last night, Esther," was Lady Brown's first speech. The chaperon's main goal in life was to awaken her niece to the many excellencies of Joshua Ramsay and Heath Abbey. Esther was disappointed to realize her breakfast was going to be ruined by a lecture. "Did he remain long?"

"No, not long."

"You should have called me. He is too nice to have prolonged his visit when you were alone. We don't want to give him the notion you are behaving improperly."

To avoid the subject Esther said, "He didn't mind, Auntie. Is there any news from the inn?" The servants visited back and forth often and kept the ladies informed of events.

Lady Brown, being an excellent gossip, was diverted to this new subject with no trouble. "I was out for a little stroll along the Thames before you came down. Such a lovely day! I happened to bump into one of your guests." This was French for saying she'd spotted an interesting client and gone tailing after him. Her niece required no translation. "He's a navy fellow, a young lad just lately back from Canada. Fletcher is the name, Beau Fletcher."

"A decent-seeming sort?" Esther asked, jealous for her inn's reputation.

"Top of the trees. Well to grass. You need not fear Mr. Fletcher will lower the tone."

"What is a naval man doing here? I wonder."

"He is ex-navy, looking about for a place to buy, he mentioned. Or a business to put his money into. He must have plenty of it. He hired the west tower suite for a week, while he looks around the countryside."

"I didn't realize the navy was so profitable. He must have made good prize money. What was his rank?"

"Captain. He would have been admiral if he had stuck with it, I don't doubt. He seemed very bright."

Esther poured coffee and asked, "How old is he?"

"Youngish. His wealth is inherited, I believe. At least he didn't mention prize money. He was regretting he had not been here two years earlier, and he would have bought your land, Esther. It is about the size he has in mind. We got chatting, you know, when he found out who I was. It would not do for *you* to chat to a young fellow, but when you reach my years, there is no harm in it." Lady Brown never found any harm in ferreting out gossip.

If Beau Fletcher had in mind a thousand acres of prime land and a home to be built besides, he was certainly well to grass. "Was Mrs. Fletcher with him?" Esther asked nonchalantly.

"He's a bachelor."

"It's odd he would not set up his estate where

he was born and bred. What part of the country is he from?"

"Northumberland. He has some affairs in London that keep him from home. He imports furs and lumber from Canada."

"I see." Mr. Fletcher became more interesting by the minute. Esther meant to discover his appearance for herself while at the inn. Any gentleman who had half his hair and was neither blind nor halt was considered young and handsome by Lady Brown, if he was civil enough to let her engage him in conversation.

It was not long in occurring to Esther that a gentleman traveler would eat in her public dining hall. If she were there, it was possible she might have Mr. Fletcher presented to her, as he now knew Lady Brown. "What do you say we take dinner at the Arms this evening, Auntie?"

"We're about due for it," she agreed. Lady Brown always enjoyed eating out, surrounded by a lively crowd, instead of sitting alone with only a niece for company. The chef at the Arms was unexceptionable, which was an added inducement.

"What's on the menu tonight?" Lady Brown asked.

"Roast beef is always on. There might be some spring lamb—I'm not sure Buck ordered any. Then there will be seafood, if you prefer that."

"With a raised pigeon pie and a slice of ham, we shall be well fed," she decided, considering the menu.

After breakfast Esther went over to the Arms and had Flame saddled up. She didn't make Mr. Fletcher's acquaintance, but she did see a handsome young gentleman hopping into a dashing black carriage, and heard a groom say, "Shall I exercise your mare, Mr. Fletcher?" She also heard Mr. Fletcher reply, "If you will be so kind," and saw him behave with that civility to inferiors that marks the true gentleman.

Her new client was indeed a handsome specimen. He was outfitted in city style, with a closely cropped Brutus' do, just brushed forward over his temples. His jacket of Bath cloth sat well on his lean and muscled frame. Esther saw only a profile of his face, which made her eager to see the rest at dinner that evening.

Dinner did not turn out as expected at all. The first letdown was that Mr. Fletcher was not in the dining room. There wasn't a decent eatery in town other than the inn. The man must have gone a few miles down the road to Windsor, which annoyed her. Another vexation was that the roast beef, her chef's best dish, was overcooked. It was as dry as day-old bread.

Lady Gloria Devere swanned into the room, dragging a trail of ancient shawls behind her. Wool paisley vied with stripes and chiffon flowers. From the sagging tendons of her neck hung her sole piece of jewelry, a string of pearls. Her skin was the same pale hue, almost transparent. Her russet hair had faded to the indeterminate shade of yellowed linen and was thin on top. Without her title she would have been small ornament to the inn. Esther spoke loudly in greeting. "Good evening, Lady Gloria."

The dame stopped by their table for a word. "Chilly this evening," she said in a quavering voice, with a hitch of the paisley scarf. "I'm afraid you'll find the beef was just a teensy bit dry, Miss Lowden. At the castle Papa used to feed the end pieces to the servants." Her rheumy eyes scanned

Esther's plate for comparison. "I stopped by Mr. Ramsay's office just now to tell him, but there was no answer when I knocked."

"I shall take Cook to task for it," Miss Lowden assured her.

"And perhaps you could tell Mr. Ramsay my windows are due for a washing. The traffic raises such a dust, but there, I cannot expect the amenities of my late father's castle at an inn." She smiled imperiously and left.

Lady Gloria was always catered to. Her unprepossessing appearance added nothing to the establishment, and as she had come to cuffs with her entire family, there was no hope for any business from them, but still, it was pleasant to be able to mention Lady Gloria when speaking of the inn.

Esther and Lady Brown went to Buck's office to deliver her complaints and to catch up on the day's doings. "Were you out, Buck?" Esther asked. "Lady Gloria said she got no answer."

"I spotted her coming and locked the door," he confessed. He told them all the little happenings at the inn. A tiff between a couple of the maids, a lost serving platter. "It's likely sitting right on the shelf. Nell couldn't find water in the sea." A string of fish-scale pearls left behind by a customer, and what should he do with them? "Fish-scale," he said, nostrils quivering. "I look forward to the day we can turn *her* sort from the door."

It was nine-thirty before the ladies rose to go home. Buck was lively company. There was some manliness lacking in him, but he would make anyone a wonderful husband, and he made Esther a competent manager. He was a good oiler of upset clients and as suspicious as a housewife of any shortage in the wine cellar or pantry.

"I'll call one of the boys to accompany you ladies home," he said, when they were ready to leave.

Just as they stepped into the lobby, they met Joshua Ramsay coming in the door. He seldom visited the inn. It "broke his heart" to see the fine old mansion sunk to entertaining travelers and to realize the family was now beneath reproach. His brows went up, and his nostrils pinched in displeasure to see Esther issuing from the office door. It flashed into her head that he was going to cut her, but in the end he bowed briefly and said goodevening.

Lady Brown gushed forward to make him welcome, but Esther adopted a stiff, formal tone to repay his hesitation. "To what do we owe the honor of this visit, Mr. Ramsay? You arrive a trifle late for dinner," she said coolly.

"I am just returning from London and decided to stop for a bite to save my servants the bother of cooking at this hour."

"You're brave, tackling the heath after dark. Go on into the dining room. They're still serving, but I advise you away from the roast beef. It's dry as dust. Buck and I have just been ordering a new stove for Peters."

"I shall accompany you home first," Joshua replied. "You *are* returning home now, are you not? Or had you planned to join the muslin company in the tavern?"

Lady Brown emitted an audible gasp. Esther was extremely annoyed with him, especially as a new guest had just come downstairs and stood listening. From the corner of her eye she noticed he was done up in the first style of elegance. He was tall and dark—her first thought was that he was Beau Fletcher, but she soon realized her error. He was not quite that tall or dark or handsome. "You will find no lightskirts here," she informed Ramsay. "If that is what brought you, you came to the wrong place. You ought to have stopped at the Black Knight. I hear they cater to men of your kidney."

Joshua knew by the glint in Esther's eye that she was about to become impossible, and he changed his tune. "What do you think kept me so late, Esther?" he asked, and laughed at her surprise.

Her attention wandered again to the newcomer, and she noticed he was staring at her, surprised at such warm talk. He looked the sort of client she wished to attract to the Lowden Arms, and for him to witness an unseemly argument in the lobby on his first night vexed her. On the other hand, Joshua's bold remark could not go unchallenged. "I see I am behind the times! Perhaps I should ask Buck to hire me a few females."

"Esther!" Lady Brown's eyes bulged in shock.

Ramsay's lips opened to object, and Esther continued speaking to forestall him. "I'll be sure to tell him where I got the idea. Perhaps you could suggest some lightskirts, Josh, from among your broad acquaintance with the species?"

The presence of a few customers in the lobby was all that prevented him from reading her a lecture. He just shook his head and laughed uncomfortably. "It will be a wonder if you don't end up in the suds, the way you carry on."

"I made sure you thought I was there already."

"Come along, I'll take you home. I shan't enjoy dinner, wondering what you're up to if I leave you here."

He offered one arm to Lady Brown, another to

Esther, and they proceeded to the front door. Before they had gone two steps, the door opened and an extremely bedraggled couple came staggering in. The man carried a hat whose crown was torn loose. He held a handkerchief to his left eye, and there were signs of blood on his shirt. The woman was completely distraught. "Help! Someone help us! We've been robbed," she gasped just before falling in a heap at their feet.

The hem of her skirt was well dusted. Her slippers also bore signs of rough usage. Her whole toilette, once stylish, was in disarray, with her hair tumbling down and her hat askew.

"What happened?" Joshua asked the man.

"A highwayman—the one they call Captain Johnnie," he said, then bent over his wife. The newcomer, who had been lurking at the foot of the stairs, darted forward and lifted the swooning lady to save her elderly husband the effort.

"The office," Esther said, pointing to Buck's lair. The man carried her in as easily as though she weighed nothing, and she was a hefty lady. Esther, following behind, noticed his broad back and his well-cut jacket. "Put her on Mr. Ramsay's sofa," she told him.

The man laid his burden down gently. "Some wine—feathers to be burned. Perhaps Miss—" He looked a question at Esther.

"Miss Lowden. I own the inn," she said, admitting the truth in the excitement of the moment. "Buck, some wine."

Buck darted for wine, Esther rang for hartshorn, and the victim's husband hurried forward to chafe his wife's hands.

"I'll send for a doctor," Esther said to no one in particular.

When she went for a footman, the newcomer followed her. After the footman was sent off, the stranger remained outside the office with her. "Perhaps it would be better if we did not clutter up the lady's sick room," he suggested. "I am Mr. Meecham, a guest in your inn."

"I'm afraid we're giving you a poor opinion of our hospitality, Mr. Meecham."

"Not at all. Offering help to distressed victims is admirable."

Mr. Meecham proved, on close examination, to be congenial. It was difficult to decide his exact attraction. He wasn't spectacularly handsome or anything of the sort. He was tallish, with dark brown hair, friendly brown eyes, and a good face, but it wasn't a face to keep a lady awake nights. Yet his combined features seemed somehow to amount to more than their discrete parts. Esther's first suspicion that he was a trifle high in the instep proved unfounded. There was a spark of liveliness in him.

"I was referring to the little argument you overheard in the hallway," she admitted. "Mr. Ramsay is a neighbor and dear friend. We rally each other and sometimes get carried away."

He smiled forgivingly and quit the topic. "I fear that poor old lady has fallen victim to Captain Johnnie. What a plague the man is. It's shocking that nothing's done about him. I have to travel the heath often myself and go in trepidation of my money—to say nothing of my life."

Esther, listening closely, sensed a good customer, if he traveled this way often. "Shocking," she agreed readily. "I should see how the victim is doing."

Lady Brown exited from the study at that moment. "She's come to," she announced with an air of relief. "It was Captain Johnnie's work, certainly."

"I shall speak to Bow Street next time I'm in London," Mr. Meecham said firmly. "They should step up the patrols on Hounslow Heath."

Esther presented him to her aunt. Lady Brown seemed unimpressed, perhaps because she was busy looking around for Mr. Ramsay. "Where is Joshua? He was going to take us home," she reminded her niece.

"The tall gentleman you were speaking to?" Mr. Meecham inquired. "I noticed him leave the hall as we came out of the office. I believe he's dining now."

Esther's anger was on the point of boiling over, to be so ill-treated in front of a handsome young client. To add to her mood, Lady Brown went into one of her tirades.

"You have given him a disgust of you, loitering about the inn at this hour, talking broad. And how are we to get home?"

"I would be happy to escort you," Mr. Meecham offered at once. "I'll call my carriage."

He wasn't to be left with the impression that they were carriageless. "We only live a step away. A footman will escort us," Esther said.

"Jack's gone off in the gig for a doctor," Lady Brown pointed out.

"Good gracious, there are a dozen boys running around."

"But I would be very happy to escort you," Mr. Meecham insisted.

The talk during the short walk was all about Captain Johnnie. Mr. Meecham won Lady Brown's favor by his condemnation of the Royal Scamp and promptly lost it again when he hinted that he would be honored to be allowed to call on the ladies the next day.

"Very kind, but we never receive strangers, Mr. Meecham," Lady Brown said firmly.

Unfazed, he replied, "Then I shall return to the inn and see if I can render any service to the unfortunate couple who were set upon by the highwayman."

"How very kind. Thank you, Mr. Meecham,' Esther said warmly, for she thought Lady Brown was rather exceeding her authority. And besides, Mr. Meecham was really very attractive.

When the ladies entered their saloon, Lady Brown immediately began to berate their escort. "That is the very sort of incident that gives Joshua a disgust of your running the inn, Esther. How contrary it is that he should have come bounding in just as we left."

"If he had escorted us home as he said he would, this incident would not have occurred," Esther pointed out. "Mr. Meecham was very polite. I think you were a little short with him, Auntie."

"A gentleman does not consider himself on calling terms only because he has lent a hand in a little emergency, my dear. You do not have the advantage of having been presented and having learned the niceties of polite behaviour. I daresay in the country such jumped-up manners pass, but they do not do at court."

"Well," Esther pointed out, "we are not at court, and *I* think Mr. Meecham was well behaved."

Before they fell into any further altercation, Lady Brown retired, just mentioning that she would not be undressing for an hour, and if Mr. Ramsay happened to stop by en route to the Abbey, she would be available to play propriety. As Mr. Ramsay didn't stop by, Esther soon went to her own room.

Chapter Three

It wasn't till the next morning that Joshua Ramsay stopped at the dower house, and to the surprise of both ladies, he was accompanied by Mr. Meecham. Lady Brown blushed and said, "Why, Joshua, I had no idea you were a friend of Mr. Meecham."

"As it turns out, we have several mutual friends," Joshua explained, "though we didn't meet till this morning when I went to the inn to hear about Captain Johnnie's latest victims. Mr. Meecham was at Harrow with my cousin and knows some of my cousins from Devonshire as well."

"We're delighted to welcome you, Mr. Meecham." Lady Brown smiled and sent off for coffee, to make up for the preceding night's curt dismissal.

Mr. Meecham displayed not the least offense. "We thought you might be interested to hear about the victims—Sir Charles and Lady Higgins," he said.

"We have been on thorns all morning," Lady Brown confessed.

Joshua took over the telling of the story. "The reason the couple arrived on foot at the inn is that Captain Johnnie, after relieving Sir Charles of his purse and his dame of her jewels, set their horses free. The horses bolted, leaving the couple stranded on the heath."

"Then it cannot have been Captain Johnnie," Esther exclaimed. "He would never be so ungallant."

"A gallant thief is a contradiction in terms," Joshua informed her. "You might as well say a clever moonling, or dark sun, but it will take a wart on his nose or a squinty eye for you to admit the man's a yahoo. He didn't find as much blunt as he hoped to, and the wife had very few jewels about her. Only a little watch and her wedding rings. He poked the crown out of Sir Charles's hat, thinking he had something hidden in it, then dumped the contents of his wife's reticule on the ground. That is when he discovered she had her diamonds sewn into its lining. In revenge he made them turn their horses loose, and fired off a shot to be sure they didn't linger nearby. He held his gun at Sir Charles's head, so there was no arguing with him."

"It doesn't sound like Captain Johnnie. He makes the men crawl under the carriage. Did he harm Lady Higgins at all?" Esther asked.

"Not really," Joshua said. "He pulled her out of the carriage pretty roughly and shoved her aside when he took the reticule from her, but he didn't strike her. At least he did not add insult to injury by kissing her, as he has the reputation of doing."

"I take issue with that!" Esther objected. "Robbing Lady Higgins of her kiss was the worst insult he could have devised. I daresay her age, not much below sixty, might account for it."

"It's a wretched mistake to glorify villains," Mr. Meecham declared.

As Esther studied him, she noticed that despite his handsome face and flashing brown eyes, he had something of Joshua's stiff and authoritative manner. "Was the highwayman alone?" she asked. "They say he travels alone—foolish of him, if he does."

"There was no one but himself," Meecham told her. "He has it down to a fine art."

There wasn't much to add to the story. The constable had been called and waited till daylight before venturing on the heath to look for clues. "The carriage had been relieved of its luggage during the night," Joshua said, "but no one holds the Royal Scamp responsible for such low pilfering. He is not the only robber on the heath by any means. The team was gone, too. It was an expensive night for Sir Charles. I'm going into London to pester Townsend to set up a heavier patrol on the heath. There should be notices in the press as well, for travelers not to tackle the spot unguarded. England has come to a fine pass when the only recourse is to limit the freedom of the innocent."

"Be sure to add a line in that notice as to where travelers can find a good meal en route, Joshua," Esther said.

"If you call stone-dry beef a good meal," he riposted.

"I most particularly hinted you away from the beef! How exactly like you to order the one dish I told you not to."

The visit was brief, but before it was over, one item of interest was accomplished. It happened right after Joshua mentioned that Mr. Meecham was taking lunch with him at the Abbey. Mr. Meecham was cordially asked by Lady Brown how long he was putting up at the inn, and when he mentioned a few weeks, he was invited to call on them.

"Why, thank you, ma'am. Now that we are no longer strangers, I shall avail myself of your kind invitation." He bowed and shot a triumphant, laughing smile at Esther. It was a look that spoke volumes. It revealed to her that Mr. Meecham possessed that necessary item, a sense of humor after all. Best of all, it hinted at an interest in getting to know her better. And though the smile didn't convey it, the fact that he was putting up at the inn revealed him to have some money.

"A little holiday, is it?" Lady Brown inquired, her nose quivering for news.

"More than that. I am doing a little business on the side, if I can persuade Joshua to indulge me."

The ladies were naturally interested to hear more. Joshua gave a quelling look to Meecham, who was looking at Esther, and remained oblivious. He continued, "We are going to have a look at the Pilchener place this afternoon."

Before Lady Brown could phrase a question, Joshua rose and said, "We'd best be going now, Meecham."

The only person left with whom she could discuss the mystery was her niece. "What business could Joshua and Meecham have in common? Pilchener's place is up for sale, but it's *huge*," Lady Brown said. "Joshua could never afford to buy it. Perhaps Mr. Meecham is more interesting than we thought. He does not *look* rich," she added, revealing what caused the new interest. "I wonder if he will buy Pilchener's estate."

After a fruitless discussion Esther decided to take a stroll by the Thames, with her prettiest parasol to protect her face from the sun, a shawl against the cool breezes, and her best morning gown in case she chanced to meet Beau Fletcher. It was there that she finally made his acquaintance.

She became aware he was following her as soon

as she began her turn along the gravel path that edged the river. When she stopped to look across at the far side, where a pleasure craft was being put into the water, he stopped a few feet behind her. When she progressed to admire the swans, he did likewise. When she continued her stroll, he was not more than two steps behind her. There was a barge in the water, towing some abandoned craft. It made an excuse to stop and let him pass, for she was curious to observe him, as he had been observing her.

Instead of passing, he stopped and raised a telescope to look at the barge. That was unusual enough that it seemed natural to look at him. Before he had it at his eye for two seconds, he took it down and looked at her, then held up the telescope, as though to offer her a look.

"She seems to be listing to starboard," he said, in the casual way of strangers who had met by chance.

"I wonder what's the matter with it," Esther answered with mild interest. Of course there was more than mild interest in her bosom.

Mr. Fletcher proved very handsome on close examination and seen head-on. If a talented young lady sat down with paint and brush to put her dream lover on canvas, she would come up with something very much like Mr. Fletcher. He was tall and dark, his complexion weathered to tan from the elements. Knowing him for a retired sailor, Esther credited his interesting shade to the wind of stormy seas and the sun of tropical climes. His eyes were a bright blue, glowing with health and animal energy, and with perhaps a hint of flirtation to add the coup de grace. Even his tailoring improved on closer inspection. His superfine jacket fit like paper on the wall, an effect achieved by only the best London tailors. His shirt was immaculate, starched to a *T*; a waistcoat of finely striped blue and yellow covered his chest. He was tall and rather slender— *elegant* was the word that occurred to her. If his lips opened to reveal a gap-toothed smile, it would be a crime.

"Her!" he said.

"I beg your pardon?"

"We call ships *her*, not *it*. They are temperamental, hard to command, yet worth every effort— obviously feminine." He smiled. No gap marred his perfect smile.

"You sound like a sailor," Esther replied innocently.

"Mr. Fletcher, formerly captain of the HMS *Glory*." He made a military bow, but with more grace than most military men could muster. Even his voice was unexceptionable—deeply resonant, with the ring of authority in it.

Such sticklers as Joshua Ramsay would raise a brow to see the introduction being carried out without the presence of a mutual acquaintance. Esther assuaged her conscience that the name of Lady Brown would soon be in the air between them to lend propriety.

She smiled and nodded in acknowledgment of his speech, but did not return the compliment. Undeterred, he pressed on with trying to discover her name. "Would you like to have a look through this?" he asked, proffering the telescope and using it as an excuse to come closer.

She said, "Thank you," and raised it to look at the barge, which was of no more interest to either of them than a leaf hanging on a tree. "I can't see very well," she said, and handed it back.

"You have to adjust the lens," he explained, and

pulled off his York-tan gloves. His gloves were lovely, his hands more so, the fingers long and tapered, well manicured. He fiddled with the protruding rings and handed the telescope back. Their fingers brushed, lending an unexpected tinge of intimacy to the endeavor. Esther's parasol was in the way, and he took it from her with another smile. She looked at the barge long enough to denote some interest before handing the glass back to him.

He looked out on the water with his unaided eyes now. "They're hauling her to dry dock to be re-rigged, I fancy."

"Very likely," she agreed, and turned to leave, but she knew the meeting was not over."

"Aren't you forgetting something?"

"What? Oh, my parasol! Foolish of me."

"Will you allow me to carry it for you?" he asked, and took a step, assuming that the answer, though tacit, was affirmative.

They proceeded past the end of Lowden Arms territory, and Esther decided to tease him a little. "Are you in the habit of trespassing, Mr. Fletcher?"

"On your time, do you mean, ma'am, or on your patience?"

"On my property."

"But I am a guest at the hotel," he answered, wrinkling his brow in confusion.

"This particular stretch of the river walk does not belong to the hotel. It belongs to that brick house up there," she said, and indicated the dower house, up several yards from the river. "And the house belongs to me."

"You must be Miss Lowden!" he exclaimed. "Where there is a will, there is a way, you see. I noticed you didn't offer your name when I so civilly gave you mine. Now I possess it without your help.

Your umbrella, your name—next I shall be stealing your heart," he cautioned, in a joking way.

"Are you a mind reader as well as a thief?" she asked, in the same spirit.

"Neither one nor the other, I promise you. We have a mutual friend, Miss Lowden. I had the pleasure of meeting your aunt yesterday morning during my stroll."

As Mr. Fletcher was proving an unexceptionable flirt, Esther decided to let the acquaintance continue. "I hope you are finding everything satisfactory at the inn," she said.

"I like it excessively. I had an excellent dinner there last night."

"Last night?" she asked swiftly.

"No, I'm mistaken. Last night I dined at Windsor. It was the night before last."

"I happened to dine at the inn myself last night," she explained, lest he take the notion she already knew his itinerary.

"I understand more exciting things transpired at the inn last evening. I heard at breakfast there was a robbery."

"Not at my inn! It happened out on the heath. The couple came here on foot. I wonder how poor Lady Higgins goes on."

"She was full of vinegar at breakfast. The center of attention, all the guests commiserating with her. No, that's not quite true. The younger ladies were jealous as green cows. It was the infamous Captain Johnnie who robbed her, they say. I don't know how people can be so foolish as to cross Hounslow Heath alone at night."

"It was ill-advised. They must have been in a great hurry to get somewhere, I suppose."

"They're going to be mighty late. Sir Charles has

35

just gone to the hiring stables to rent a team. That was gratuitous infamy on the Scamp's part, to cut the team loose and make those poor old folks walk five miles in the dark of night."

"Hardly what one would expect of an officer," she agreed. "They say Captain Johnnie is an ex-army man, you know."

"It's hard to believe an ex-officer was responsible for last night's escapade."

"You don't think it was Captain Johnnie, then? I tend to agree with you."

"That was not my meaning. No doubt he is responsible. What I meant to say was that he never was an officer. He is a cowardly knave, a thief, and a robber."

"I stick to my guns. Captain Johnnie would never treat a lady so shabbily," she argued. "No doubt he is given credit for more robberies than he commits. That's what is turning him into a legend. By the time Lady Higgins gets to her destination, she will be convinced not only that it was the Royal Scamp, but that she is in love with the rogue—be boasting of having attached him."

"I shouldn't be at all surprised. With my own ears I heard her story change three times over breakfast—and I'm a fast eater, too. First he was a scoundrel who roughed her up; then he was at least not so ungentlemanly as to have touched her; then, as I paid for my coffee, he had kissed her, just before he darted into the night, cape flying. She'll have had an offer of marriage before she gets home, certainly. That is how these legends spread."

"Like so many of the world's wrongs, it is the fault of ladies, in fact!"

"You are stuffing words in my mouth. A wish to cut a dash is a human failing, not restricted to the ladies. We seem to have reached the end of the gravel walk, Miss Lowden. Do we turn around and go back, or may I escort you home?"

"And rob me of a chance of being waylaid by the Royal Scamp?" she asked.

Mr. Fletcher gave a dashing smile and replied, "If it's only a kiss you're after, we don't require a highwayman for that! On the other hand, I cannot undertake to relieve you of your gold. I draw the line at stealing hearts."

Esther was surprised to see how swiftly an accomplished flirt could forward an acquaintance. She knew, however, that Mr. Fletcher's conversation infringed on the borders of fast behavior and gave him a haughty stare. "I suggest you draw your line somewhat closer to the realm of propriety, Mr. Fletcher," she advised.

"Hmm," he said, smiling from the corners of his flashing eyes. "Your reprimand is in order, ma'am. I shall withdraw to higher ground."

Esther hesitated a moment, trying to decide whether to stomp off in a huff or leave the door open to further dalliance. His startling blue eyes were a strong inducement to the latter course. They continued walking, and after a moment she said, "Higher ground sounds more like an army term than a naval one. I should have thought a sailor would retire to safer waters."

Mr. Fletcher's reaction was peculiar. He gave a conscious start but soon recovered. "I was mixing my metaphors, ma'am. I am half a layman by now, you see. All we stuffy gentlemen take high ground on propriety between the sexes. I daresay it would be too forward of me to suggest we go for a drive this afternoon. Sticking strictly to high ground, of course. I have a spanking team of bays." His bold smile proved more tempting than the team of bays.

He saw her waver. "Such a lovely day," he continued. "It cries out for a turn along the river. Twickenham is not far away. We could visit Strawberry Hill."

"What a rare treat! I haven't been there above a dozen times."

He laughed lightly. "I should have known better. I've only been here a day, and already I have visited the Gothic wonder. It's the first spot folks go, I should think."

"One is allowed to visit either Windsor or Strawberry Hill first without offending the proprieties. You are a fast worker. You did both the first day."

"I only dined in Windsor. It is still to be toured, but I dare not suggest such a well-worn pastime to you, Miss Lowden. I shall have to think up something more original. What a charming little house," he exclaimed as they drew closer to the dower house.

"Thank you. We like it. And now that I am safely home, I shall leave you." Esther didn't want Mr. Fletcher to find her too easy to conquer. No more was said about their driving out together. She was willing to wait a day and see what original pastime he came up with.

It was an hour past lunch when Buck Ramsay called to discuss the new stove for the inn, and afterward he remained for a chat. Lady Brown didn't feel her presence was necessary at these dull business meetings and was out harassing the gardener.

"Lady Gloria was complaining about dust under her bed. The old malkin couldn't see an elephant with a spyglass, but she can spot a flake of dust at twenty paces," he complained. "Jennie had just been up there with a dustmop. The girl's about as much good as a cold in the head."

"Is there any more word on the Higginses?" Esther asked.

"They've left. The constable is pestering our clients. I'm letting him use my office so that newcomers don't take the notion they will be subjected to a questioning. It gives the place a bad reputation. That Mr. Fletcher, for instance, was in the boughs at being quizzed so thoroughly, and he, you know, is taking the expensive tower suite by the week."

"Was he singled out in particular by the constable?" Esther asked with quickened interest.

"It happened he arrived back at the inn not long after the Higginses. He looked pretty unkempt when he came in. Lady Higgins took a look at his dusty jacket and boots and squealed, 'That's him! That's the man who attacked us!' Of course she came to her wits and apologized, but it got the constable's suspicions up."

"Why was Fletcher covered in dust?" Esther asked, her own suspicions rising at this story.

"He lost a wheel coming home from Windsor and helped his driver repair the rig. The wheelers are all closed at night, you know, and as he was close to home, he managed to recover the wheel and hold it on the shaft with a green bough, just for the last mile."

After a frowning pause Esther said, "That's odd! He invited me to drive out with him this afternoon. He couldn't get a wheel replaced so quickly, could he?"

"I expect he could if he had sufficient reason," Buck replied with an arch smile, hinting that Miss Lowden was sufficient reason for anything.

Esther was not above flattery, but she wasn't a fool, either. She remembered Mr. Fletcher's condemnation of Captain Johnnie and his insistence that it was the Royal Scamp who had harassed the Higginses. Surely he wouldn't have done so if he were Captain Johnnie himself, and if he had no alibi. Then there was the odd business of his using an army term when he claimed to be a navy man— and Captain Johnnie was said to be an army man.

"Buck," she said, jumping to her feet, "send a groom out to the stable to examine Mr. Fletcher's carriage. See if a wheeler's been to the stable today to fix that wheel, and let me know the answer immediately."

"You actually think he might be Captain Johnnie?" Buck asked, his eyes staring from his head.

"It's possible. And if that wheel wasn't damaged, I want you to turn Mr. Fletcher out of the inn. Good God, he could be rifling my guests' rooms this very instant."

"Egad!" Buck said, and tore from the house.

He was back within a quarter of an hour. "Fletcher did have a breakdown. Old Judge Mortimer was passing on the road and saw him, just about the time the Higginses were attacked. The wheeler was at our stable this morning, repairing the wheel."

"That's a relief!"

Buck shook his head. "It is, and it isn't. We have a new suspect. All a hum, I daresay, but Lady Gloria waylaid me again. She haunts the lobby like a ghost. Says she saw Meecham climbing up a ladder into his room last night—he's next to her, you know—a while before the Higginses landed in. Her fear—or hope—is that he was after her poor old body. Good God, Methuselah wouldn't take a sec-

40

ond look at her. Mounted on a fast goer, though, Meecham would have had time to stash his loot and still reach the inn before the Higginses arrived."

"Meecham? But he's a friend of Josh's."

"No, an acquaintance. They only met at the inn this morning. I heard Meecham introduce himself."

"We must warn Josh! And we must keep a sharp eye on Mr. Meecham," Esther decided. "If I'm found harboring Captain Johnnie, there isn't a lady or gentleman in England will put up under my roof."

"I don't know about that," Buck said, rubbing his chin. "Plenty of folks would relish the idea. If we could capture him, you could have a Captain Johnnie suite and charge something extra for it."

Esther stared. "I cater to quality, Buck, not to Cits."

"But how can I keep an eye on him?"

"Does he travel with a valet?"

"No, his groom tends to his clothes as well. A sort of general factotum."

"Like a batman, you mean, as the army officers use," Esther said. Her voice suggested the significance of this.

"Mr. Fletcher and several other gentlemen are doing the same."

"I wish we had a better quality of guest. Well, if Meecham has only a groom, you can look around his room sometime when he's out, for his groom will be driving him, and the room will be empty."

"You don't think he'd hide the loot in our inn?" Buck asked.

"He has to hide it somewhere."

"By Jove!"

Buck ran back to the inn, and upon learning that Mr. Meecham was out, he darted straight up to his room, where he found no missing loot, but only a

41

spill of grease on the carpet and a white ring under an empty wine bottle. These signs of slovenliness, while outrageous, didn't seem worth another trip to the dower house, so he sent Esther a note. She couldn't decide whether she was relieved or disappointed when she read it, but she meant to continue a close surveillance of Mr. Meecham. She must discover, for instance, whether he had a mount in the stable, and what sort and color.

Chapter Four

Esther seldom honored Mr. Joshua Ramsay with
a visit unless she was invited, but she felt the matter of Mr. Meecham's behavior was important
enough to have the horses put to. Immediately after lunch she and Lady Brown drove over to Heath
Abbey. Even without her aunt's yearning sigh Esther realized how lovely the estate was. As they
drove through the park, she admired the green of
spreading beech and oak trees, varied by soaring
conifers. In the distance a long facade of stone was
visible between the trees. Dormers, gables, and
chimney stacks punctuated the skyline. Long windows gleamed like diamonds in the sunlight.

The butler welcomed them and led them into a
small saloon, done up in elegant blue velvet and
brocade, with carved chairs and tables. Soon Joshua
came in, looking every inch the country gentleman
in his buckskins and topboots.

He first welcomed Lady Brown, then turned a curious eye on the younger lady. "Well, Esther, are
you cadging money for the orphanage, or has the
roof of the Lowden Arms fallen in? I know you never
honor me with a visit without a good reason."

"Sorry to disappoint you. The roof still stands,

43

and I'm not after money. I've come to talk about Meecham."

Ramsay lifted an imperious brow. "What about him?"

"It is possible he's Captain Johnnie."

A bark of laughter rang out. "Good God, Esther, your brain has turned soft. If you suspect one of your guests is the Royal Scamp, I suggest you look in a different direction. Buck mentioned a Mr. Fletcher. I didn't see his phiz last night when the Higginses landed in, but if you recall, Mr. Meecham was there."

"Fletcher dined at Windsor and had some trouble on the way home. He was seen at the time of the robbery, in fact—by Judge Mortimer. About Meecham, the Scamp possesses a horse, a large, dark stallion according to gossip. One assumes it could have got Meecham to the inn long before the Higginses, as they were forced to walk five miles."

"It's impossible. I know the man's family."

Esther reined in her temper. No other surety was required if Joshua knew the family. It was the very sort of toplofty speech that annoyed her. "What odd acquaintances you have! Is the entire family in the habit of entering houses by means of a ladder up to their bedrooms? That was Mr. Meecham's mode of entry last night. Lady Gloria saw him."

"That foolish old woman," he scoffed. "She has Buck up looking under her bed two nights out of three, hoping to find a man lurking there. Wishful thinking."

"She is not senile! I expect she knows a ladder when she sees it."

"A servant cleaning the windows probably left it there."

"The windows were not cleaned yesterday. And

she saw Meecham climbing in. I think he is the Royal Scamp. You are our deputy lieutenant. What should be done about it?"

"Keep your foolish notions to yourself, or Meecham will have you sued for slander," he advised.

"Is that all you have to say?"

"Not at all. I mean to offer you some refreshments. Wine, or coffee?" He pulled the cord and ordered coffee.

Lady Brown disliked to disagree with Mr. Ramsay, but she was considerably perturbed. When the servant left, she cleared her throat and said, "Perhaps you could just look into it, Joshua. You mentioned entering some sort of business deal with Meecham. You would not want to find yourself mixed up with a thief." Her brightly curious eyes invited an explanation of this very interesting matter.

"Our business is nothing that lends itself to chicanery. I want to buy Pilchener's place."

"That huge estate!"

"Yes, well the house and buildings are grandiose, and of course I have no use for another house. It happens Mr. Meecham wants a weekend pied à terre in the country near London. I want him to buy the house, and I'll take the land. Mr. Meecham, on the other hand, wants me to buy the whole estate and he'll rent the house."

"Has he no money, then?" Lady Brown asked.

"He's not high in the stirrups. Younger sons seldom are, but he has a good position at Whitehall and enjoys country living."

"It is a handy location for a highwayman" was Esther's contribution. "Rented, too, so he could nip off when the law began closing in on him."

Lady Brown had other thoughts. How did it come

that Joshua was suddenly in a position to be buying Pilchener's place? His father used to say he was land rich, cash poor. "You inherited some money, did you, Joshua?" she asked.

"Not at all. I have merely improved production here at the Abbey since my father's death. Naturally I'd get a mortgage for Pilchener's place. I have been wanting to enlarge my holdings for some time." An accusing look at Esther reminded her what estate he had lost out on.

The coffee arrived, and Esther poured. She admired the heavy silver set and the dainty china. Everything at the Abbey was fine. She had been reared to rule such a place as this and when she came here, she always felt how far she had fallen. Beyond the windows acres of park, dappled by sunlight, spread as far as the eye could see. She fell into a reverie, imagining herself living here as Joshua's wife.

When she shook herself to attention, she realized Joshua was gazing at her while her aunt rambled on in her chatty way. "Wool gathering, Esther?" he asked.

"Just thinking."

"From that wistful expression, I'd guess you were dreaming of the Royal Scamp."

A flush colored her cheeks. Was it possible that thinking of marriage to Joshua made her look wistful? No, it was just the lovely Heath Abbey. "Mr. Meecham does not interest me. I had thought Captain Johnnie would be more dashing."

"I daresay he is. Meecham is a deputy secretary in the attorney general's office."

"You really think he is innocent, then?"

"I'm convinced of it, but I'm happy you suspected him. It's not often you call on me. Don't feel you require such an extraordinary excuse next time. I don't have many social calls these days."

"That might be because you so seldom entertain, Joshua. Last year you used your father's death as an excuse not to hold your annual ball. What is your excuse this year? I haven't heard you mention resuming the custom."

"It is the lack of a hostess that deters me. A large house such as this needs a mistress."

Lady Brown smiled benignly on her niece. "That is true. Esther loves to manage such affairs as a ball."

"What prevents you from having your own ball at the Lowden Arms?" he inquired, not quite innocently.

It was enough to get Esther to her feet and enough to set Lady Brown scolding all the way home. "You should have been more conciliating, Esther."

"Why should I, when he wouldn't even listen to what I had to say? He knows Meecham's relatives—that is enough. If the scoundrel decides to murder half my clients, I shall be the one held to blame."

"You see what happens when you open your house up to the public. It is the riffraff that come storming in."

As they neared home, Esther said she would drop in to see Buck, and Lady Brown was let off at the dower house. Lady Gloria was in Buck's office, with a new complaint. "The milk at lunch was a wee bit off," she said. "It gave an odd taste to the tea. Likely the servants left it off the ice last night. I know how hard it is to get servants to do things right, none better. We had eighteen servant girls at home." She rose, hitched up her shawls, and smiled. "You won't forget to have my windows washed, Mr. Ramsay? This is the second time I have asked you. I like to sit by the window and take a peek out from time to time while I read. It rests the eyes."

"Silly old ass," Buck said, when he had closed the door behind her. "But a good payer, of course. I'll set a lad to cleaning her windows. It is only the company she wants. The cream was fine."

Esther soon got down to more important business. "I spoke to Joshua. He says Meecham is innocent."

Buck rubbed his chin pensively. "He may not be Captain Johnnie, but he did have the ladder from the shed last night, or someone did. It was left outside the inn. Demmed odd, eh?"

"Put it in the cellar," Esther advised. "He'll not get in that way again. I have half a mind to turn him off. Tell him the rooms are all taken. On the other hand, he works at Whitehall and could be a good advertisement for us."

"We'll keep an eye on him."

"A sharp eye, Buck. Let me know if anything else unusual happens."

As Esther went into the lobby, she met Mr. Fletcher just coming in. "Miss Lowden! Come to check up on your minions, I see. May I escort you home?"

Mr. Fletcher's smiling face and pleasant attitude, not disapproving of her business venture, were a welcome change from Joshua. "I would be happy for your escort. You must wonder how it comes that I am running an inn," she said.

"Not at all. I have sufficient knowledge of the world that I can surmise the cause. Your father left his estate encumbered. You're an enterprising young lady and rescued yourself. So many would have been satisfied to live on the remains of their capital. How can ladies settle for such monotony? I wonder."

When they were outside, Mr. Fletcher drew in the fresh air and said, "Ideal weather for a drive. It is not at all late. . . ." He looked for her response.

"Very well, a short ride. You were to come up with a novel idea, Mr. Fletcher," she reminded him.

He summoned a groom and sent for his carriage. "As you have placed Gothic windows, ramparts, towers, and noble walks on the interdict list, we shall visit a lesser-known historical site instead."

"We are to tour Mr. Pope's formal garden at Twickenham," she said with resignation.

"That's out, too, is it?"

"I don't know for a certainty that I have ever seen it on April the twentieth before," she said thoughtfully. "But time limits us to a short radius."

"Not all that different from April the nineteenth, I warrant. You would have seen it any number of times on April the nineteenth. We'll go to Ham House instead. Or is it also as well known as an old ballad? You limit my ingenuity by curtailing me to a short radius."

"I see what it is. You want to feel water rolling under your feet again, Mr. Fletcher."

"If you can call the Thames water," he said disparagingly. "I am more accustomed to the mighty Atlantic. The Thames does not roll; it glides."

"Where did the Atlantic roll you? Are you one of the heroes who protected us from Napoleon?"

The carriage came, and he assisted her into it before answering. "Unfortunately my past is less glorious. I was sent to North America, to defend Canada from the revolutionaries to the south."

"What was it like? Was it very wild? Did you see any Indians?"

"I met a few. They're savages," he said, and laughed. "What was it like? Well, it was very cold and very hot. They don't warn you it will be hotter than the hobs of hell in summer. We all went equipped with blankets and fur jackets, and landed in the middle of July into a tropical climate. But the sun wasn't too bad. It was pretty well obscured by black flies and mosquitoes."

"I see you had a marvelous time."

"It ill becomes an officer and gentleman to complain, unless he is on the point of remedying the situation. Otherwise it is mere carping. The sun is beyond my control. It was wonderfully broadening. Travel always has that advantage, if no other. But for me it also had the advantage of enriching me financially, so I shan't say another disparaging word."

"Was there good prize money?"

"No, good opportunities. Tall timbers practically being given away, and as to the furs! I import them both."

It was only a short dart down the road to the Twickenham ferry. There were half a dozen tourists making the trek to Ham House. They made a brief tour of the island, admired the octagon room of Orleans House and the daffodils along the route. The sun shone warmly above, and the scenery was very poetic. The day was too fine to spend time touring indoors. They went back to the White Swan for high tea. It was a modest spot, but the tea was excellent, or seemed so with Mr. Fletcher for company.

"Next time I'll hire a boat and we'll row along the bank, chasing the swans," he said when they stood at the railing of the ferry that carried them back to Twickenham.

"You sound as though you mean to make a long stay in the neighborhood."

"A man has to live somewhere. I like this area as well as any I've visited."

"That is odd! Mr. Meecham, another guest at my inn, is also looking for a house nearby. We are becoming very popular."

Fletcher gave her a flirtatious glance. "I wonder what can account for it? This Meecham—who is he? What does he do for a living?"

"He works at Whitehall."

"Odd, his staying here."

Esther wished to learn more about her companion and said, "Where are you from, Mr. Fletcher?"

"Northumberland, the beautiful Lake District. I'm a younger son. My brother inherited our family home. He has a wife and two children now. It will be more convenient for me to live close to London," he said. "I couldn't bear to live in the city, though, with nowhere to go to get away from it. I'm a country boy at heart."

"Won't you miss your family?"

"My parents are dead. It is only Cathy I miss—that's my younger sister. I do miss her." His face wore a sad, nostalgic smile when he spoke of her. He sang her praises for a few minutes.

"Is it just a country home you're looking for—something close to London—or do you want an estate, a farm...?"

"I sound an utter fool, but I'm in the curious position of not knowing what I want. Since leaving the navy, I feel at loose ends. I'm a partner in this importing business in London that takes about one day a week. I like London, enjoy that one day, but

I want to live in the countryside. I think I want to do more than just have a house, but I'm really not at all knowledgeable about farming. I hesitate to put a lot of money into an enterprise at which I'm a Johnnie Raw. You're a businesswoman, Miss Lowden—what do you advise?"

"I always advise everyone to open an inn." She smiled. "It has served me very well. Or do you think it beneath you, as some of my friends think it is beneath me?"

"I have already told you, I admire your initiative. I don't consider it infra dig by any means. Well, I am already in commerce, so there could be no stigma in it for me. Perhaps you can tell me a little about your business—show me around your inn."

"I'd be happy to. Is the importing business profitable?" she asked, as one businessman to another.

"Extremely, but I am only a junior partner in the company. The pity of it is, I sold my idea and contacts to a fellow just before . . . The thing is, I hadn't much capital at the time, but have inherited some money from an uncle since then. I could buy my partner out, but then I would have to spend so much time in the city, and I don't want that. You see my dilemma. I'm cash rich and idea poor."

"I hope you don't expect pity for that! You are to be envied."

"I'm not complaining—only discussing my life with a friend who has got her own in such superb order. You're something quite out of the ordinary, you know." His eyes lingered a moment on hers. She felt a flush of pleasure, but still, it was too soon for any more intimacy, and she called him to order.

"Help me think about it," he ordered. He tucked her hand into the crook of his elbow for a stroll along the deck and behaved with perfect propriety for the rest of the trip.

It was close to dinnertime when they reached home. Lady Brown was miffed at Esther's lengthy absence, and she was not much appeased when Buck arrived at nine for his nightly meeting. He had sustained a visit from an old friend who was in the hotel business and had a few ridiculous suggestions with which to plague Esther.

"Mr. Moss stared to see our limited menu," he said, before he had been seated long. "He is with the Pulteney at the present time. I blushed to my eyebrows when he asked to see the list of French dishes. 'None, Mr. Moss,' I confessed sadly."

"With our new stove, perhaps we can add some to the menu," she consoled him.

" 'Not even a *sauté de poulardes à la Provençale*? All the crack in London,' he told me. 'No *saumon au beurre de Montpellier*? No *filets de volaille à l' Orléans*? Good gracious, what *do* people eat when they put up here?' I could not even suggest he try our speciality, the roast beef. It was bone dry again." Buck shook his head sadly.

"We are not competing with the Pulteney, the most lavish hotel in the city, Buck," she pointed out.

"Indeed, no! I begin to wonder if we are even competing with the Black Knight and the street vendors who peddle kippered herring on street corners. Then, to have to confess the dessert menu was equally limited. A good dessert might have saved face. And what did I have to offer him? An apple tart—what you would be served at any country table. I shall have Peters try a *nougat à la Française* this very week. Mr. Moss mentioned it. And perhaps a *croque en bouche aux pistaches* for the gentlemen. We really do require a pastry chef, Esther. They have six at the Pulteney."

"Perhaps in the future."

A smile split Buck's face. "Ah, I meant to tell you!" he said. "We have a duchess with us this evening. The Dowager Duchess of Gresham, with a whole retinue of hangers-on. They've taken eight rooms in all. Three carriages sit in the stables, one of them with strawberry leaves and another with a lozenge on the side. Fortunately Mr. Duval's party had vacated the east tower suite, and I could offer it to her grace." A look of beatific joy infused his face at the magical title. "She liked it amazingly. It reminded her of a suite in Lord Petersham's country place. I don't doubt we'll have Petersham and his set here before the year is out. Some boxing match is spoken of nearby. All the smarts and swells attend such affairs. I don't know how they can bear the brutality, but certainly bruisers enjoy a great popularity." He shook his head at this anomaly, for Buck disliked to be at odds with the ton about anything.

"When is the meet to be held?"

"Sometime in May. We'll begin to receive requests for reservations any day now. Every room for miles around will be booked in advance. There will be a handsome profit for us. Pay for the closed stove and perhaps even a pastry chef in one weekend."

Pleased with his news, Esther went along with him. "There's nothing to be gained by stinting. You have to spend a sprat to catch a mackerel."

"A wise philosophy. I can think of no greater joy than acting as host to the ton, unless it is to be paid for it. The best of all possible worlds, as that admirable Frenchie said—what was his name? The *Candide* fellow."

"Voltaire."

"That's the chap. We don't want it whispered in London that we are behind the times. And while we are discussing improvements, Esther—that carpet on the upper floor is in rags."

"Why, the nap is hardly off it."

"It's the lower class of client who uses the upper floor—they are hard on carpets. They drag their feet along like old drays."

"Then the old carpet is good enough for them." Buck sat trying unsuccessfully to think of a counterargument. "What is Meecham up to this evening?" she asked.

"He is out. We'll keep our ears cocked to hear if Captain Johnnie strikes."

"And Mr. Fletcher, is he also out?"

"He was in the card room when I left."

"If Johnnie strikes tonight, we'll know it was Meecham. Well, our suspicions will be strengthened at least."

Buck soon left. Esther kept listening for the sound of the knocker, thinking Joshua might stop by, but he didn't, and at eleven she retired.

Chapter Five

There was no report of an attack by Captain Johnnie that night. At breakfast the next morning the servant brought Miss Lowden a note, not delivered by post but sent over from her inn. It was from Mr. Fletcher, reminding her in polite words of her promise to show him around the inn, and inquiring when she might be free to do it. Rather impatient to see Mr. Fletcher again, Esther sent a reply saying she would meet him at the inn at ten o'clock.

Lady Brown had a few words to say about this. "The man has the behavior of a commoner, Esther. Taking you over to Ham House yesterday without sending word home to me where you were. I was considerably worried about you. And now this. Why does he wish to see the inn?"

"He wants to open a business himself, Auntie."

A quick smile lifted Lady Brown's lips. "And is he thinking of buying the Lowden Arms? What a blessed relief it would be to have the place off our hands. Joshua would be thrilled to death."

"He didn't mention buying the Arms. Of course I gave no indication it is for sale. I wonder if that is what he has in mind. . . ."

The Lowden Arms was not officially for sale, but

with her aunt and Ramsay forever telling Esther it made her ineligible, she thought of selling it from time to time. The idea was in her mind when she put on her pelisse and straw bonnet with a clutch of cherries flirting over the brim, to go to meet Mr. Fletcher.

He was awaiting her in the lobby. His tall, lean form lounged elegantly against a pillar. He hastened forward when he saw her. "Punctual as well as beautiful!" he complimented.

Esther, delighted with the compliment, gave a playful smile. "We business folks are accustomed to punctuality in our meetings."

She noticed that Mr. Meecham was hovering about the desk, using the pretext of glancing at the morning journals, but she took the idea he was listening to them. As he didn't look up, however, she didn't acknowledge seeing him. It occurred to her that Joshua would not be long in ignorance of the meeting, and she felt a little pleasure mixed with her annoyance.

"Where shall we begin the tour?" Fletcher asked.

Mr. Meecham's head rose. Soon he walked forward. "Miss Lowden. Nice to see you again."

"Mr. Meecham." Her greeting was not curt, but it did not encourage further speech.

"I couldn't help hearing you mention a tour of the inn. Would it be too encroaching of me to attach myself to the party? I have a great fondness for these old and stately homes."

Esther saw a sparkle of mischief in Fletcher's blue eyes, and lauded him for his quick-wittedness. "Tour of the inn?" he asked, frowning. "I'm afraid you misunderstood, Mr. Meecham. Our tour is of the village. Miss Lowden has kindly agreed to show me the shops. Such a fine day—what we are really after is an excuse for a walk."

Mr. Meecham looked a little embarrassed. "That will teach me to eavesdrop!" He laughed.

"Yes," Esther said, smiling but rather mockingly.

She and Fletcher walked from the inn, to lend credence to Fletcher's lie. "What a mushroom the man is!" he scoffed.

"Why, because he wanted to tour my inn?" she teased. "Take care what you are about, sir. Meecham is not the only gentleman who has asked that favor! Perhaps he wishes to buy it. I told you he is looking for a house. It's Meecham I should be giving the tour. You are merely curious," she said, and looked sharply for his response.

It could hardly have been more gratifying. "You mean you would sell! It would suit me right down to the heels!"

"I'm not eager to sell, but I might consider it if the price were right."

While they dallied along the walk, Mr. Meecham's mount, a dark horse but not black—it was a deep chestnut with a white blaze on the forehead—was led to the door. He mounted and cantered down the road toward Heath Abbey. Mr. Meecham rode well and made an attractive figure as he darted along, with his wide shoulders limned against the horizon.

Watching the direction of Esther's interest, Mr. Fletcher said, "A penny for your thoughts. You don't have to tell me. I was just thinking the same thing myself—that Meecham fits the general description of the Royal Scamp. Those shoulders have a fine, military look. One can't help overhearing rumors, you know. Lady Gloria Devere has been whispering in rather a loud voice that Meecham uses a ladder to enter his chamber. Have you given any thought to turning him off, Miss Lowden? A few of the clients were wondering if you would."

"I cannot like to do it. He is a good friend of Mr. Ramsay—not Buck but Joshua Ramsay, a local worthy."

"I did just wonder, when he was so eager to attach himself to our tour. The Royal Scamp might have some interest to learn all the nooks and crannies and hiding places of your inn."

"Oh, dear! You're giving me the megrims, Mr. Fletcher. You don't suppose that's why he wanted to join us."

"I don't ignore the more obvious reason, that he wanted to enjoy your company, as I do. Perhaps you should ask your manager to keep an eye on him." She nodded, worried. "Now that he's gone, shall we proceed with our tour and see if we can come to terms?"

"I haven't said I'd sell. The inn is a very profitable, going concern. I would expect a stiff price for it. All my renovations and two years' work must be taken into consideration. Goodwill and so on. The location, too, is attractive."

"Spoken like a true Cit," he said, the sting softened by a charming smile. "What price did you have in mind?"

"I haven't given it serious thought at all. It's just an idea that occurs to me from time to time."

"It would be best if you mull it over for a few days," he suggested. "There's no hurry on my part. Naturally you will display every reluctance in order to raise the price, and I will be at pains to disparage all your finery to lower it."

"So that is how gentlemen conduct business with a lady, is it?" she asked archly.

"Why, ma'am, it goes without saying, ladies don't conduct business. It is their indifference to turning a guinea that makes them ladies—and dead bores."

There was little formality between them after this interlude. "We might as well begin with the kitchen, as you are familiar with the dining room," Esther mentioned.

Mr. Fletcher had a keen mind and was swift to see advantages and disadvantages. From the kitchens and the cheese and storage rooms under the eaves to the wine cellars, they toured it all, omitting only the rooms occupied by guests. Mr. Fletcher jokingly found fault, and Esther praised every doorknob and window.

"Do you have any secret panels, any priest's hole, or that sort of thing?" Fletcher asked.

"Nothing so romantic. Not even a ghost, unless you count Lady Gloria Devere."

"The old shawl-draped lady? She has an ethereal air about her. One would never take her for nobility."

Mr. Fletcher went along, tapping at walls and testing cupboards. "You have a deal of waste space here," he pointed out as they walked through the airless attic storerooms. "If you pitched out this lumber, you could turn this area into half a dozen small rooms."

"I do not feature small rooms here; I run an elegant establishment," Esther replied.

Mr. Fletcher looked around at the trunks that lined the walls, the broken chairs and accumulation of rejected household objects. "There are occasions when you could rent a cubbyhole or cupboard for a decent rate. The boxing match next month, for instance—fellows will pay an arm for any place to lay their heads at such a time. If I know anything, you'll end up having bodies here, sleeping between the trunks."

"I think not," Esther objected. "That would crowd the dining area and cause a ruckus in the stable and lobby."

"You don't plan to use this space during the match, then?"

"Only for storage."

"You're giving spiders free rent," Fletcher told her, as he brushed a cobweb from his shoulder. He was soon shoving trunks aside to search for secret panels.

"You're wasting your time, Mr. Fletcher," Esther said. "There are no secret panels, no ghosts. Really a very dull building when you come down to it."

"What size of a wine cellar do you keep, Miss Lowden?" he asked.

They went to the kitchen and got a brace of candles before descending to the wine cellar to admire the dusty bottles and black beetles scuttling into dark corners. "Is there just the one doorway to reach the cellar?" he asked. "What I am thinking is that wine could easily be stolen if there is access from outside."

"There's no outside door," she assured him. "Just the one from the pantry and one from my manager's office, which used to be the butler's room. I don't worry that he is stealing from me; he may have any wine he wants without asking. That's about it," she said when they finished touring the cellars.

"You haven't showed me the door to your manager's office," he reminded her.

"It's in that little passage behind the hogsheads," she said, and pointed it out.

Mr. Fletcher had to see it for himself, test the door, and would have gone up to Ramsay's office if Esther hadn't stopped him. "You'll give poor Buck heart failure," she warned. "No one uses that door but him."

They returned upstairs. "You will have seen the grounds and stable yourself," she mentioned.

"Would you mind pointing out to me how much of the land belongs to the dower house, and how much goes with the inn? I noticed you keep your mounts at the inn stable," he said. "Do you not have a stable at the dower house, Miss Lowden?"

"Not a usable one."

"Then you would want to keep enough land to build one. You won't want to pay stabling fees at the inn after you sell it."

"I'm sure we could work out something on that score. There's a derelict barn out back," Esther mentioned. "The lot could be divided to include that tract with the dower house. I didn't get a formal severance, as I owned both properties."

"I don't remember seeing any stable near your place."

"It's overgrown with vines. There's a tall thorn hedge between it and the house. It hasn't been used in decades, as the dower house wasn't occupied."

"I expect you won't want to go tramping through wet grass in your dainty slippers. We'll do that another time. May I walk you home, Miss Lowden?"

As they walked along the path to the dower house, he first thanked her for showing him the inn, then said, "How many acres go with the place?"

"I kept ten, including the dower house and its land. Say eight at the maximum for the inn."

"It doesn't leave much room for expansion," he pointed out.

"But on the other hand, you wouldn't be paying for land that stands idle, and you might be able to buy up a few more acres from neighboring properties if you want it in the future."

"I see I'll get no bargain from you, Miss Lowden," he bantered.

"No, indeed. My being somewhat reluctant to sell prevents that."

They reached her door, and Mr. Fletcher bowed himself away, promising he would call soon to continue bargaining.

It was only half past eleven, and Esther decided to change into walking shoes and rougher clothing to go over her land and see how much of it she should maintain for the dower house. Renovating the old barn might be cheaper than building a new stable. She was becoming excited about the possibility of selling, but her eventual plans didn't involve living year-round in the dower house. It would be only a summer home, while she rented a flat in London for the dull winter months. Perhaps some obliging relative might even find her a parti. . . .

Esther wrapped herself in last year's pelisse and put on her oldest walking shoes for the short trip. Once she was off the beaten path, the tall grass hampered her walk. The barn was so overgrown with vines that only its roof was spotted between the trees, and thorn bushes had sprung up along the way. She'd have to cut a new path to the barn if she decided to turn it into a stable. Her hem was wet with dew by the time she finally reached the structure.

It was a low, spreading building, stone at the bottom, with the top finished in lumber. Whatever paint might have once decorated it had long since worn away, leaving weathered wood that looked rather pretty peeping out behind the vines. She took a step through the broad opening into the dark, cool space. There was no wooden floor, just damp earth underfoot. The earth and the vines at the window openings gave her a feeling that she was not in a building at all but in some leafy glade. Sunlight filtering through the perishing roof completed the effect. But what was it that lent that feeling of eeriness? A definite shiver tingled up her spine. Some sixth sense told her she was not alone in the deserted building, and her heart pounded.

As her eyes adjusted to the dimmer light, she looked to the far corners of the barn but didn't advance farther into the building. What was that shadow? It moved, and her heart leapt to her throat.

"Did I frighten you? I'm sorry, ma'am."

Esther swallowed her heart as a tall shadow detached itself from the far corner and advanced toward her. It quickly took on the form of a man. "What are you doing here, Mr. Meecham?" she demanded.

He stepped into the light, smiling sheepishly at being caught. "Merely satisfying my curiosity," he said. "When I learned Mr. Fletcher was touring the inn, I assumed it was with the intention of purchasing it. If it is for sale, I am interested as well."

"Who said Mr. Fletcher was touring the inn?"

He gave her a laughing look that caused the light in his brown eyes to dance most attractively. "I am neither deaf nor blind, Miss Lowden. After a short ride I returned to the inn. I saw the two of you coming down from the attics and entering the kitchen. But please don't be embarrassed at having conned me. Actually it was Fletcher who told the lie. You were only an accessory after the fact."

Esther felt a warm flush suffuse her cheeks. "It was a business tour. I didn't know you had any business interest in my inn, or you would have been welcome to join us. I expect Mr. Fletcher wanted my total attention. Naturally he had a great many questions to ask."

"What sort of thing was he interested in?"

"Everything," she said comprehensively.

"Secret passages, that sort of thing?"

"That possibility always arises in these ancient houses."

"And does the Lowden Arms have any such features?"

"No, it hasn't. If I'd realized there was such an interest, I would have had a few installed while I was renovating."

"It has plenty of space at any rate. This barn might be turned into a dance hall for guests at the inn."

"I hardly think so. Only servants dance in barns."

"Horn and hoof, Miss Lowden," he said, wagging a shapely finger at her. "The farmer's creed, but it ought to be followed by us all."

"But you're not a farmer. Mr. Ramsay mentioned you were looking for a private house only."

"That's true, but my being a gentleman farmer's son makes me alive to farming possibilities."

"Where does your family farm?"

"In Devonshire," he said vaguely. "It will screw Fletcher up to a good price for the inn if he thinks he has some competition."

The truth of this was not slow in registering. Esther began walking around the barn. "I had thought I might rebuild this into a stable for myself," she mentioned.

"I hardly think it warrants rebuilding. The roof is shot."

"But the walls are still quite stout," she said, and went to examine them more thoroughly.

She had the impression Mr. Meecham wanted to stop her investigation. He didn't try to do it by force, but when she headed for the west corner of the barn where he had been hiding, he distracted her a few times by pointing out spots in the wall where light came through, and mentioned the lack of a hayloft.

"I don't intend to keep a commercial stable, Mr. Meecham. A pair of carriage horses and a mount for myself is all I would require," she said, and walked briskly to the far west corner.

In the loose earth there were fresh horseshoe marks, traces of oats, and the lingering aroma of animal. "It seems the poachers use this isolated spot," he said. "I've noticed small game is plentiful. There's a wine bottle with the dregs still wet, in the corner here."

Esther had already spotted the gleam of glass and picked the bottle up to read the label. "This comes from my inn!" she exclaimed. "It's our most expensive brand."

"Really!" Mr. Meecham said, and took it from her. There was an air of excitement about him that she couldn't account for. "Are you sure?"

"Of course I'm sure. My manager buys this from a London firm. None of the locals use it, so far as I know. And poachers certainly couldn't afford it."

"Perhaps someone had a picnic here."

"It's hardly suitable for a pleasure walk," she pointed out.

66

He smiled warily. "For some pleasures, men prefer seclusion." She frowned in perplexity. "I am speaking of petticoat dealings," he added bluntly. "A footman or groom might be aware of this private oasis."

"My footmen and grooms don't have mounts. There's been a horse or two here as well. I don't like this, Mr. Meecham."

"What is it you suspect?"

"I—I don't know," she said, and was suddenly taken with an anxiety to leave. What she suspected was that Captain Johnnie had hidden his mount here. The bottle of wine told her Captain Johnnie was a guest at her hotel, and common sense pointed to Mr. Meecham as the culprit. Common sense also whispered that if he realized the direction of her thoughts, he might detain her—permanently.

She hastened to the doorway, afraid he'd stop her, but he only followed quickly at her heels. He didn't realize she suspected him, then, and she must be cautious not to alert him. Once back in the sunlight, her fears faded somewhat, and she tried to behave normally.

"What you have is two sets of trespassers," Mr. Meecham explained. "Poachers using horses, and errant footmen meeting their light-o'-loves for trysts."

"That would explain it," she agreed quickly.

"What will you do?" he asked.

Her mind raced to find the most clever answer. "Probably nothing but put a lock on my wine cupboard," she said airily. "I don't mind the poachers thinning out the rabbits. The place is overrun with them, and as to the footmen—why, I suppose they will meet their girls somewhere, and they bother no one at the barn."

She looked closely at her companion as she mouthed this lie and didn't think she was imagining the relief she saw there. She'd alert the constable to keep an eye on the barn, and with luck, Captain Johnnie would be in irons after his next holdup.

"Generous as well as beautiful," he said approvingly.

Meecham accompanied Esther back along the path to the dower house. Newly leafed bushes in blossom scented the air, the sky was an azure arch above them, and birds warbled their mating calls, but this spring beauty went unnoticed by Esther. It was all she could do to keep from breaking into a run in her eagerness to get away from Captain Johnnie. When they encountered an overgrown tangle of bush and weeds, he stepped in front of her.

"Let me go first and break a way through the bush for you," he offered.

Once they were past this barrier, the more cultivated garden of the dower house was reached. The backhouse boy was working on the cucumber hills, and with her own servant nearby, Esther felt she had reached safety.

They stopped and looked back over the wildflowers that bedizened the grass and up at the pattern of trees against the sky. A calm satisfaction settled slowly on Meecham's face as he gazed around. "It's very beautiful, isn't it?" he asked softly, as though speaking to himself. "Almost like a little Garden of Eden, cut off from the world. You can't even see the inn from here or hear it. I wish I could throw up a little hut here at your back door, camp beside the Thames as we used to camp along the Tag— Tamar when I was a boy."

The scenery and his idyllic description had lulled Esther into calmness, but she looked sharp when he stumbled over the name of that river.

Meecham quickly spoke on to distract her. "The company in those days was not nearly so charming or so beautiful," he said, with a conning smile. Not the real smile of earlier; the mood had changed.

"Camp along the Tagus" was what he had started to say. That river was well known from the Peninsular campaign. Any bivouacking Meecham had done had been in Spain or Portugal. He was an army man like Captain Johnnie. She studied his complexion. It was weathered, not tanned dark like a newly returned officer's. No, he had been home from the Peninsular War for a few years. And Captain Johnnie had been ruling Hounslow Heath for eighteen months.

Esther found herself staring into his dark eyes. She might as well have spoken her thoughts, for the knowledge in his was easily readable. His conning smile faded; a quick frown pleated his brow when he realized she'd noticed his slip. It was followed by a questioning look, doubtful, soon settling to knowledge. All these changes occurred in an instant. Before another instant had passed, a reckless, rakish smile flashed, and Mr. Meecham pulled Esther into his arms.

He crushed her against his chest, and his lips came down hot and hard in a scorching kiss. She made a futile attempt to push him off, but it was like a kitten fighting a tiger. He easily overpowered her and held her for a long embrace that, strangely, began with a ruthless attack and eased to gentleness as Esther stopped struggling. When he released her, she gazed mutely at his darkly dilated eyes. He wasn't smiling triumphantly, and he

69

wasn't angry. He looked rather startled, and so did she.

She pulled away, her cheeks flaming from the unexpected interlude. "I'm sorry, Esther—Miss Lowden," he said.

As she glanced down, she noticed he was still holding her two hands in his. "You'll be giving me the idea you're the kissing bandit, Captain Johnnie," she said. Her voice was unsteady, but her gaze was firm. He didn't flinch or try to deny it.

"I knew what you were thinking. Since I was suspected of such villainy, I foolishly decided to play the part. It was rash. I do apologize."

"I will expect you to check out of the inn immediately," she said.

"Don't be so foolish," he scoffed. "I'm not the Royal Scamp."

Esther lifted a haughty brow. "Are you not, Mr. Meecham? Still, I would prefer not to take any chances. And it *does* give the clients an odd impression to see guests clambering into their rooms by means of a ladder, you know."

His brow lowered in anger. "I haven't done anything. The only way you can make me leave is by blackening my name, and if you do that, you'll open yourself to an expensive slander suit."

"Mr. Meecham! *You* are the one who is foolish. You can't go on using the inn now. I know who you are. I'll notify the constable. You'll be watched incessantly."

"A fine scandal that would cause. Miss Lowden, proprietress of the Lowden Arms, *claims* to have caught the Royal Scamp. Why, you'd be immortalized with a ballad before a week was out. Is that what you want, to be a byword in the taverns? No, Miss Lowden, you may be slightly eccentric, but I can't believe you want your name broadcast so indiscriminately. I think you will keep your suspicions to yourself. That's all I ask."

"Don't try to intimidate me," she said, and strode angrily away. She resisted the urge to turn around when a low rumble of laughter trailed after her.

Chapter Six

Esther wanted to discuss Mr. Meecham's suspicious behavior with someone more sensible and worldly than her chaperon, yet she hesitated to take her story to the constable. Neither a lawsuit nor a scandal involving her inn was desirable. Joshua Ramsay was the logical person—older, worldly, presumably wiser, and Mr. Meecham's surety. But Joshua was in London, and besides, she didn't want to give him the satisfaction of knowing she was in a hobble. His cousin Buck couldn't be relied on to keep it quiet from Joshua, either. Within ten minutes it occurred to her that Mr. Fletcher was a possible confidant, and within fifteen she had sent a note to the inn requesting him to meet her by the Thames.

He came promptly, his blue eyes agog with curiosity. "Miss Lowden, what is the matter?" he asked. There was a noticeable air of concern about his handsome brow; he possessed her two hands and gripped them tightly.

"How kind of you to come," she said, and squeezed his fingers as tightly as he held hers.

His concern softened to a smile. "You knew I would" was all he said, but the simple words suggested a high degree of devotion. "Now tell me what has got you hipped, and we shall sort it out."

"It's about the Royal Scamp and Mr. Meecham." They began a slow turn along the gravel walk, and Esther emptied her budget to him, explaining all her suspicions, but skimming rather lightly over Meecham's physical attack on her. "It's intolerable that he is staying at the Lowden Arms, rubbing elbows with respectable people like yourself. Is there no way I can get him out without causing a scandal or laying myself open to a lawsuit?" she asked.

Mr. Fletcher gave her fingers an avuncular pat and considered the matter a few moments. They sat on a wooden bench at the end of the walk. It was situated behind a stand of ornamental shrubbery that provided privacy. "I think I know what you should do, Esther," Mr. Fletcher said at length. "I— I hope you don't mind my calling you Esther?" he asked apologetically. "It slipped out."

It seemed hard to insist on the formalities when she had sent for him, and she graciously consented. Soon she agreed to call him Beau as well. "What do you think I ought to do?" she asked.

"Let him stay."

"Let him stay?" she exclaimed. "My whole purpose in sending for you was to discover how I might turn him off."

"Turn him off if you like; he won't set up a revolution. If he is Captain Johnnie, he doesn't want publicity any more than you do. That was mere bluster. He shan't stay long now that you've tumbled to his identity, but as long as he is here, it gives us an excellent opportunity to observe him. With luck we might even capture the Royal Scamp. That would be quite a coup for your inn."

Esther beamed a dazzling smile on her companion. "How clever you are!" she exclaimed. "But we shall need help, Beau. We can't capture him by ourselves. And I would rather not ask for Joshua's assistance. He's so arrogant, there's no bearing it."

"I have my groom."

"If you need more men, you could recruit some footmen or stable hands at the inn," she offered, and gave him a few names.

It was settled satisfactorily between them that Beau would watch Meecham like a hawk and follow him if he left the inn after dark. "I believe I'll dine at the inn again tonight," Esther said before leaving.

"Please don't. I don't want you in harm's way, in case anything happens. And besides," he added with a bantering smile, "it gives me an excellent excuse to call on you this evening to make my report."

This gallant answer sent Esther home with a smile on her lips and a rising heart. It wasn't till a rather tedious afternoon had been got in that she realized she was missing out on all the excitement. It was only the anticipation of Beau's visit that evening that kept her at home.

To her dismay, when Beau came, he was accompanied by Joshua Ramsay, hot from London. It turned out the gentlemen had come separately and met on the doorstep.

"I've spoken to Townsend," Joshua said. "He is setting up two-man patrols every mile along the heath. Five miles of heath, five sets of two men. It should do something to ease the current rash of robberies."

"Any news in town?" Lady Brown asked.

"I heard a Mrs. Fineway was relieved of her reticule, but it wasn't the Royal Scamp's work. He wouldn't bother with her plain old black carriage. He specializes in robbing the well-to-do. He seems to know that his victims are well inlaid, and traveling with money and jewels."

"I expect he hangs about at some popular inn and keeps an eye on who's leaving," Beau said. He didn't look at Esther, but she knew the remark was a slur on Meecham.

"Yes, some such spot as the Lowden Arms," Joshua said with a satirical grin.

"It serves the nobility right for blazoning a crest on their carriage doors—an open invitation to theft," Esther claimed.

Joshua lowered his brows and stared at her. "Do you consider it an invitation to be molested when a pretty lady displays her charms in a low-cut gown? You misplace the blame to put it on the victim."

"Touché." Esther smiled. "Something has sharpened your wits, Joshua. You don't usually speak so much to the point. There were no robberies reported at my inn tonight?" She darted a secret glance toward Beau.

"It's a bit early for it," Joshua said unconcernedly.

A glance at the head-and-shoulders clock on the mantel showed her the truth of this. It was only nine o'clock. In her eagerness to see Beau she hadn't thought that his coming prevented him from guarding Meecham. Beau saw her worried look and sought a way to reassure her. When Lady Brown cornered Joshua for some quizzing of the sort elder ladies inflict on younger gentlemen, Beau moved to the sofa by Esther and said, "Don't worry about Meecham."

75

"Should you not go back to the inn?" she asked.

"My groom's keeping an eye on him. If Meecham leaves, he'll bring my saddled mount to me and I'll be after him."

Esther felt a sinking sensation. She began to fear that Beau was more interested in dalliance than in capturing Captain Johnnie. If the terror of the heath had a headstart of ten minutes, there'd be no hope of overtaking him, but she worded her objection discreetly. "That gives Meecham an advantage of several minutes."

"I don't believe he plans to go out tonight at all. He's settled into a private parlor with a group of guests, playing cards and drinking rather heavily. He's half disguised, to tell the truth."

"Not making a racket, I hope?" she asked. There was more than one way to ruin an inn's reputation, though her manager was good at handling such contingencies.

Beau reassured her and soon they rejoined the general conversation. His visit was short, and as Beau left, he indicated that he'd return to the inn and continue his vigilance.

Joshua turned a sapient eye on her. "Setting up a new beau, Esther?" he asked.

"Not at all. *New* implies there is an *old* one lurking in the background," she parried.

"I stand corrected. Setting up a beau, period. And a demmed poor choice, if you don't mind my saying so."

"I do mind, not that that will stop you. Fletcher is amusing, but he's not the only onion in the stew. What have you against him?"

"We don't know a thing about the man. He might be anyone."

"You don't know anything about Meecham, except what he chooses to tell you. It doesn't seem to deter you from making him a bosom bow."

Lady Brown stirred restively and said, "People are better off sticking with those they know." This was meant to hurl the two youngsters at each other's heads. They both ignored her.

"Tell me, Josh," Esther said, "is your Meecham an ex-army man?"

"He was in the Peninsula till he took a ball in the arm. Why do you ask?"

"I have my reasons," she said vaguely, but she was annoyed that Meecham wasn't trying to hide his background. Surely he had begun to say "Tagus" and switched it to "Tamar."

"He's reticent about his army days. Tired with everyone congratulating him, I daresay. He was quite a hero. He's a younger son from a very good Devonshire family. When he left the army, he decided to follow a political career. In fact, I mean to have him stand for parliament for this district in the next election."

"To vote for all your policies," Esther said, unimpressed. "If politics is all you can find to talk about, you should be at the tavern with all the other dull gentlemen."

"An excellent notion. I believe I will drop over and see if Meecham is there."

"He is. If you hurry, you might find him not quite foxed."

"Show Joshua to the door, Esther," her aunt suggested. Such short and discreet intimacies as this were encouraged.

"I'm always happy to show Joshua the door." Esther smiled.

Joshua acknowledged the shot with an appreciative eye. When they were alone, he said, "How does it come Fletcher is running tame here?"

"Blame it on my calling," she said, and told him about Fletcher's interest in the inn.

A smile of approval beamed. "You mean you're trying to sell it!"

"No, but I might consider it if the price is high enough."

Ramsay gave her a curious look. "What has changed your mind, Esther?"

"Greed. I have no politicians in my pocket to line up profitable ventures for me, as you have."

"True. I was at Whitehall just this morning, re-arranging the country's economy to suit myself. Actually I was talking to Sir Clarence Fulbright at the finance minister's department about Paul. I thought he might fit in there—Paul Meecham. He has a head for figures. His talents are wasted in his present position."

He opened the door but hesitated a moment before leaving. "A moonless night," he said pensively. "Captain Johnnie's favorite raiding weather. I hope some hapless souls aren't molested."

"You would rob us all of entertainment," she teased. "Why, I shouldn't be surprised if ladies take to the heath on a moonless night in hopes of a kiss from him."

A reckless grin flashed across Ramsay's face. Shadows concealed the familiarity of his features. For a moment Esther saw only the glitter of dark eyes, the flash of white teeth; then she was pulled into his arms and kissed. Surprise threw her off balance, and before she had time to object, she found herself being crushed in his strong arms, against a wall-hard chest. That the staid Joshua Ramsay should behave so daringly robbed her of reason. It was a thoroughly confusing moment, and after it was over, Esther admitted it had been enjoyable.

"I wouldn't want you to risk your safety on the heath just for want of a kiss," he said when he released her. She thought he would sound embarrassed at his unusual act. His voice held no hint of embarrassment. It was insinuating, gentle, amorous.

Esther felt constrained to declare an annoyance she was far from feeling. "That's about the poorest excuse I've heard yet," she scoffed.

"Next time I'll have a better one." He laughed and strode off into the shadows, leaving Esther alone to ponder the unusual matter. It had been a very nice kiss. She doubted Captain Johnnie could do better.

Some new atmosphere had invaded the neighborhood. Twice in one day she had been kissed. It was the shadow of Captain Johnnie that was turning all the men into these reckless romantics. If the ladies lauded him for his daring, they thought, why should they not exploit it? At least it had been both Meecham's excuse and Joshua's. And Esther was not at all sorry. Perhaps it was just what was needed to bring a tingle of excitement to country living.

Chapter Seven

Twelve hours later Beau Fletcher was back, puffed with news. In her eagerness Esther ran to the hallway when he came in. She knew by his stricken face that he had failed her.

"Not another robbery!" she gasped.

"The worst yet."

"What happened?"

"He's killed two men," Beau said. His face was pale. The news had left him weary and haggard, as though he hadn't slept. She led him to the saloon and gave him a glass of wine to buck him up for the telling.

"When I left you last night, I watched Meecham till he staggered to his room at about one o'clock in the morning," Beau assured her. "I really think you're mistaken about Meecham. It couldn't have been him. The raid occurred just before dawn. There was a shipment of gold leaving the London mint, destined for distribution to the banks in Bath. It was supposed to leave at dawn, but it left a little early and was taken as soon as it entered the heath."

"What of the guards Joshua spoke of last night?"

"It must have occurred somewhere between the postings of guards—they're a mile apart, Ramsay said."

"Was the shipment not accompanied by its own guards?" Esther asked.

"There was a small convoy, armed guard on horseback traveling fore and aft. The guards were picked off first, shot in the back from afar—a rifle, obviously."

"That sounds like a military man!"

"Make that men. The guards were shot simultaneously. Captain Johnnie's got himself a cohort. The driver survived and gave the account. While the carriage driver was still in a state of shock, the masked raiders swooped down on him from the shadows. One of them was a small fellow, the driver said. Captain Johnnie followed his usual procedure—put the driver face down on the ground and made off with a stunning load of gold."

"That wasn't taken away on horseback," Esther said. "He must have had a wagon waiting."

"No, he took the wagon, horses and all."

"It could hardly have been accomplished by two men. This is the first time he's *murdered*. There'll be some strong action from Bow Street now. Where can he be operating from? He used two mounts, and where did he take the wagon of gold? He cannot have taken the wagon to my stable, thank God."

"The Black Knight is the likeliest spot, but I'm afraid I have unpleasant news, Esther," Fletcher said. "The Bow Street runners are going over your inn with a fine-tooth comb."

"Oh, dear! I'm ruined. No one will come back after this."

"At least the runners didn't find anything. Your

guests seem to be taking it in good part. It's ridiculous to think the highwaymen would take their loot to either the Black Knight or your place—the two obvious spots. They were still close to London; they'd rattle into the city, with thousands of places to hide."

"How much did they get away with?" Esther asked.

"Ten thousand in gold coin. They certainly knew the shipment was to be made. It's odd they should have discovered it, for the government is usually at pains to conceal such information. The Scamp's a cunning scoundrel."

"Scoundrel?" Esther asked, eyes flashing. "You are too kind, Beau. He's a vicious killer, and a coward to boot. Shooting men in the back." The image of Mr. Meecham was in her mind. He was a dashing fellow, to be sure, but a vicious killer? Perhaps his stint in the Peninsula had inured him to killing. "And you don't think it was Meecham?" she asked reluctantly.

"I can't believe he got himself sobered up and halfway to London by the crack of dawn."

"He might have been shamming it, pretending to be disguised."

"I suppose that's possible. Once he retired, I returned to my room."

"Was he in his room when Bow Street arrived?"

"Yes, I followed them to his door. He was in bed, but of course there's no knowing how long he'd been there. His mount hadn't left the stable since the afternoon before, so if it was Meecham, he left the inn on foot and had his cohort meet him with a mount."

"We should have checked my old stable last night to see if he had mounts there. He didn't leave his room and return by my ladder at least, for I had Buck put it in the cellar."

Beau looked at Esther's worried face and grimaced. "I should have kept a closer eye on Meecham," he said. "I tried to stay awake but fell off into a doze around three this morning."

"Oh, Beau," she said, smiling, "I didn't expect you to stay awake all night. No one could do that. Captain Johnnie himself doesn't do it. He knows when he means to strike and takes his rest when he can. But a twenty-four hour guard must be kept on Meecham and on my stable, too. It's not your fault; it's mine. This is a job for Bow Street, not a couple of amateurs like us."

"Would you like me to speak to them?" he asked, but reluctantly.

"You don't like to impugn Meecham's character?" she asked.

"He might be completely innocent. It seems a hard thing to do."

She considered it a moment. "I'll handle it myself. I shan't make any accusations. I shall merely tell the runners what I know. I'd feel culpable if I didn't do that much. I *do* feel guilty," she added thoughtfully.

Beau reassured her, but she could see his real interest was to get back to the inn, and before long, he left. Esther sent a footman to her old barn. Nothing suspicious was reported when he returned. She felt useless, sitting in the dower house while all the excitement was going forth at her own inn, only yards away. She sought about for an excuse to go there, not just to speak to the runners but to move into the inn temporarily. Lady Brown would have to go, too, of course. That was the problem, convincing her aunt to move into that hotbed of intrigue and impropriety.

How could she accomplish it? The roof of the dower house didn't leak—that might have done it. Their servants weren't ill. The house didn't require fumigation. Esther looked about the Rose Saloon, seeking an excuse to find it intolerable. Other than looking a little old and dingy, it lacked nothing. Old and dingy—she had always spoken of redecorating it, but the inn required so many changes that all her money went into it. She had some extra now. Painting a few rooms here would be her excuse to remove to the Lowden Arms. Their bedrooms and the saloon being the most frequented, these were chosen for renovation.

Esther took the precaution of informing Lady Brown of her intentions without, of course, telling her Captain Johnnie's latest escapade. In her innocence Lady Brown sighed and said, "I cannot endure the smell of paint. I suppose we shall be tolerably comfortable at the Arms for a few days, and it will be nice to have the house freshened up. It is looking fatigued," she added, staring about the walls and ceilings. "Just give me a few days notice, and I shall be packed."

"The men are coming today, Auntie."

"Today? When did you call them?"

Esther crossed her fingers and said, "Yesterday. I'm sorry, I forgot to tell you. I'll call the maid now and have her pack for you."

Esther had a busy morning. She sent off for the local painter and harangued him into starting work that afternoon. She packed her own trunk to allow the servants to help her aunt, and by early afternoon the ladies strolled over to the Lowden Arms to select their rooms. There was a little awkwardness in making Lady Brown see the advantages of two indifferent chambers, their only merit being that Esther's room was next to Mr. Meecham's.

"We would have a better view of home from the corner room, Esther," Lady Brown pointed out.

Esther replied, "These rooms are a little cheaper, Auntie. If we leave the more expensive ones for hire, it would help defray the cost of redecorating at home."

"That's true, and we see the main road from here. That will make a diversion, to sit at the window and watch the carriages bowl past."

Esther planned much livelier diversions for herself. She darted down to the lobby as soon as her aunt was installed and went to Buck's office. "Where are the Bow Street runners?" she asked Buck.

"They've all left but Officer Clifford, and he came dressed as a farmer, to allay suspicion. What a morning it has been, Esther, and now we are saddled with a farmer, when we agreed not to entertain anything but gentility. He might have posed as landed gentry at least—not that anyone would have believed it with aitches dropped all over the place and a jacket that my groom wouldn't be seen in."

"Send for Clifford," Esther said.

Buck knew his employer had something important on her mind when she didn't throw a tantrum at housing a man who was posing as a farmer. "What's up?" he demanded. "What's brought you here to stay a few days? You never mentioned decorating the dower house, which is not to say the place don't need it. I should like to have discussed the decorating with you."

Esther quickly considered a plausible answer and said, "You have often mentioned that the Rose Saloon needed refurbishing. The painter had a cancellation, and I took advantage of it."

"I hope you saw his colors."

"Yes. I want to warn Clifford he must behave with the utmost discretion. I won't have him bothering my guests."

"It is a very pale rose I had in mind."

"Yes, yes. A very pale rose. I wish you would hurry, Buck."

"He'll do you up in a garish pink if you don't keep an eye on him. I'll take a dart over myself later."

"Fine, but first call Clifford."

Buck left and was back in five minutes. "Clifford isn't free right now. They tell me he's interviewing Mr. Meecham in his room. Giving another client a disgust of us," he added sadly. "And Mr. Meecham such a fine gentleman, too, a friend of Joshua's."

"In his room?" Esther asked quickly.

"Yes, but I daresay he won't be long. Shall we nip over and check out the painter while you wait?"

Esther was already on her feet. "No, I'll wait in my room, Buck," she said, and flew upstairs, where she put her ear to the wall to try to overhear what was being said next door. Lowden Hall had been well built. No sound penetrated through the thick layers of lath and plaster and several coats of paper. She tried the fireplace that backed against Mr. Meecham's fireplace; it was a little better. She could hear a low hum but nothing distinguishable as a human voice. Dare she go into the hall and put her ear to the door? No, that was too farouche. She looked hopefully to the window. Hers was closed, but if she opened it, and if Mr. Meecham happened to have his open ... She ran to the window and flung it open. By sticking her head and shoulders out, she could see that Mr. Meecham's window was closed tight. There was nothing to do but wait.

When Mr. Meecham's door was heard to open, she ran to her own door, and when Mr. Clifford sauntered past, she whispered to him. A cunning, wizened little prune of a face turned and stared at her from a pair of bright brown eyes. The man looked deplorably out of place at her inn. That dilapidated blue jacket was no ornament even to the farming profession, but he was an officer of the law, and Esther beckoned him into her chamber.

"I must speak to you," she said, and introduced herself.

"Ye were my next stop. Ye know who I am, then," he said, his head wagging importantly.

"Yes, indeed, and I am very grateful that you are staying here," she said politely, for she wanted to ingratiate him.

"I'm doing no more than my duty," he answered with a quiet show of modesty. "The world's as bent as the devil's elbow, and it is my job to straighten it."

"You do it very well, I'm sure. Did you learn anything interesting from Mr. Meecham?" she asked.

"As ill luck would have it, he slept through the entire affair, so he couldn't tell me if there were any comings or goings here last night. He was a trifle foxed, I believe. Certainly his room smelled like a brewery."

"Have you spoken to Mr. Fletcher?" was her

next question, delivered with such a sapient eye that the runner perked up his ears.

"Aye, that I have, miss," he said, and nodded wisely.

"Did he mention Mr. Meecham to you?" she inquired. Now that the moment was at hand, she found herself strangely loath to air her suspicions of Meecham. What did they amount to in the end? He hadn't told her he was a veteran. He had been in her barn—which was hardly criminal when he told her his reason. And he had kissed her—which she had no intention of mentioning. Ah, but there was the ladder!

"I can't say that he did, but Mr. Meecham mentioned Fletcher," Clifford answered with a sage nod. "Strange, Fletcher hanging about here with no rhyme or reason."

"He has a reason! He is looking to buy a property nearby."

"Aye, but he hasn't visited an estate agent. Claiming to be in Windsor the night the Higginses was robbed, and losing a wheel—that's a poor sort of a story."

"Mr. Clifford!" Esther exclaimed, astonished at such wrongheadedness. "You're not suggesting Mr. Fletcher is involved! The local judge saw him with his carriage broken down the night the Higginses were robbed."

"It was dark as the devil's waistcoat that night."

"Judge Mortimer identified him. It is my inn he wishes to buy. I gave him a tour yesterday."

"Now, that I find highly suspicious," Clifford said, shaking his head. "Why else would he want a tour of your ken but for to know all the ins and outs of it? Where he might stash a cache of stolen goods, or come and go as he pleases. Highly suspicious," he added. "Has he made you an offer to purchase the inn?"

"Good heavens, no. It's only been mentioned. Nothing is definite."

As Meecham hadn't hesitated to direct blame away from himself, Esther delayed no longer in redirecting it to its proper target. "Mr. Meecham was trespassing at an old abandoned barn of mine yesterday," she said. "There were fresh marks from horses there."

"So he told me. And the bottle of wine from your place, too. 'Tis fortunate he discovered that. I hope you haven't mentioned it to young Fletcher? I took a quick trot over to the barn this morning, but it wasn't used for the gold robbery. A wagon rattling in and out would have alerted you. Did you tell Fletcher about the barn?"

"Of course I did!"

"Why 'of course,' miss, if you don't mind my asking? Aiding and abetting an outlaw highwayman won't do yer reputation a deal of good."

She shook her head angrily. "You've got it all wrong," she said, and outlined the true nature of events.

Mr. Clifford listened patiently, only shaking his head at her naïveté. "Yer partiality for young Fletcher is showing, if you don't mind my saying so, Miss Lowden. I know both the lads are right in size and shape and agility to be Captain Johnnie."

"No, they're not. Mr. Fletcher is too thin."

"Jackets can be wadded out to any size. Both landed in on you around the same time as well, and both keep lurking about with no clear reason. Fletcher took a tour of the place. Why would it be you chose Meecham as your highwayman?"

"Because—" Esther came to a dead stop. After a

89

little consideration she said, "Meecham rides a dark stallion. Mr. Fletcher's mount is white."

"That's highly suspicious. It is," Clifford said.

She relaxed at his agreement, but he soon spoke on to disillusion her. "Highly suspicious that Fletcher chose a white mount. They're rarish, except in old gray nags that are white with age. Fletcher's is a genuine white mare. It certainly looks like he's trying to deflect suspicion from himself. As to Meecham's nag, if it's the dark horse stabled here he uses when he's being Captain Johnnie, what would he need your old stable for?"

"Perhaps he has two mounts," she invented. "Last night there were two men."

Clifford fixed her with a piercing brown eye. "Do ye really think Captain Johnnie's such a flat, he'd ride his working horse into public, bold as brass? Divil a bit of it."

She played her ace. "Mr. Meecham used a ladder to enter his room the night the Higginses were robbed," she said, and explained the time element.

"That is odd," he admitted. "I'll quiz him on that score. What is odder is that young Meecham was at pains to ask around who Ramsay is, and when he found out he was the prime citizen in the countryside, he suddenly decides he was at school with his cousin."

Esther came to quick attention. "Did he, indeed? I hadn't heard it. But he could hardly 'decide' such a thing, Mr. Clifford," she pointed out reluctantly. "He would need names, times—information."

"Which he was at pains to get in the tavern that same night and went strutting out to meet Ramsay next morning when he stopped by the inn. Oh, he's a cunning enough rogue, Mr. Meecham," he finished.

Seeing her runner was being more reasonable, Esther tried a new tack. "You realize, Mr. Meecham was in the army, like Captain Johnnie," she said.

"I do. Quite a hero he was. I've checked that out."

"You haven't had time," Esther said swiftly.

Clifford smiled an oily smile. "Bow Street is awake on all suits, miss. We had half a dozen lads down here this morning. I sent one of them off to check war records. Captain Meecham was in the Peninsula with Beau Douro, right enough. A fine job he did, too, by all accounts. Near got his left arm blown off, but it didn't stop him. Ah, I do like a military man," Clifford finished, sighing in admiration. "If I was twenty years younger, I'd have been in the Peninsula myself, giving Beau a hand."

Officer Clifford rose and strutted to the door, a shabby parody of a hero. "As to your Fletcher, since you're so mighty close to him, Miss Lowden, you might fish around and see if you can find out who and what he really is. Not that he'll tell you, but a clever lady like yourself might pick up on something." The words "clever lady" were delivered with an ironic smile.

"Mr. Fletcher is ex-navy, Mr. Clifford."

"The Admiralty is slower than the army to cough up their secrets. I haven't verified him yet. Not that he couldn't borrow a real sailor's name."

"The same applies to Meecham."

"There's no saying the Scamp was a military lad at all. There's always a hundred rumors about such creatures. He don't wear scarlet regimentals, and if he did, it wouldn't necessarily prove anything but he visited a costume store. Facts, Miss Lowden. That's what I'm after. Facts, not rumors. How did the Scamp learn that gold shipment was being made, for example? There's a puzzler." Mr. Clifford bowed and left the room, muttering into his collar.

Esther was so disgusted with him, she didn't know whether to laugh or shout. To think the capture of Captain Johnnie was in the hands of a fool like that was enough to sink her spirits. She wanted time to think in private and sent off for tea to soothe her addled nerves. How did Meecham discover the gold shipment was being made if it was a guarded secret? It must have been his accomplice, someone from London, who ferreted that out. *I was talking to Sir Clarence Fulbright at the finance minister's department about Paul.* Good God! Had Joshua learned of the shipment yesterday and inadvertently let it slip out to Meecham? He said, when he left her, that he was going to see Meecham. She must ask Joshua about that.

Over the second cup of tea her thoughts took a different direction. There were some striking similarities between Fletcher and Meecham. As Clifford pointed out, both were the right size and coloring to be the notorious highwayman, or could be with wadding in the shoulders of a jacket. Both had arrived at the inn at the same time, and both were remaining longer than guests usually did, both using the pretext of wanting to buy a house in the neighborhood. How could she know whether they were lying? Joshua hadn't met Meecham before this visit, and it was possible Meecham had invented the whole matter of being at Harrow with Josh's cousin.

Esther thought and thought. It occurred to her that there had been two men involved in last night's robbery, and perhaps Fletcher and Meecham were a team, calling themselves ex-soldier and sailor to confuse everyone. How they must be laughing at her if she had set one thief to watch his partner. After much earnest effort all she could think of was to follow Clifford's advice. She'd try to learn more about not only Meecham but also Fletcher.

She couldn't pursue any of her goals from her room, so she tidied her toilette and headed for the door. Glancing at the tea tray, she decided to take it to the kitchen herself, down the servants' stairs. She had just entered the hall when Mr. Meecham's door opened and he, too, left his room. He gave a start of surprise when he saw her. "Miss Lowden!" He looked at the tea tray and the door from which she had issued. "A shortage of servants?" he asked archly.

She gave an answering smile, engineered to disarm suspicion. "Not quite. I am having my saloon painted, and am living at the inn for a few days."

"Let me take that to the kitchen for you." He took the tray from her.

"Thank you. Did Joshua Ramsay find you last night? He was at my house and mentioned coming here to look you up."

"He stopped around for a moment, but as I was busy at a card game, he didn't stay long." But it wouldn't take long to mention having spoken to the Finance Department, and Meecham would pump him for any useful information. It was, presumably, the meeting with the Finance Department that Josh would have discussed with his protégé. "You've heard of Captain Johnnie's latest stunt?"

"I have. Shocking, is it not?"

"You must take care not to go near the heath after dark, Miss Lowden."

She gave him a conning smile. "And you, too, Mr. Meecham."

On this superficial pleasantry Mr. Meecham took the tray to the kitchen, and Esther set off to find Joshua, to pick his brains.

Chapter Eight

Joshua Ramsay had heard of Captain Johnnie's latest atrocity and, like half the gentlemen in the neighborhood, went pelting off to the Lowden Arms to discuss it with his colleagues. His dark brows drew together when he saw Esther tripping toward Buck's office. He went storming in after her.

"Esther, for God's sake, go home. This is no time for you to be in a place like this! Every yahoo in town is here this morning."

He was back to his usual self, all reckless charm abandoned. Esther almost felt she had imagined that romantic kiss the night before. "Why should I be different from the rest of you? It's my inn. Sit down, Josh. I was just going to ask Buck to send a footboy after you. You've heard about the gold robbery?"

"Of course. That's why I'm here."

"Did the gentleman at the Finance Department in London happen to mention the shipment to you yesterday?"

"No, he didn't. Why do you ask?"

"Just curious. I don't see how else anyone around here learned of it. I thought you might have mentioned it to Meecham last night—inadvertently, of course," she added hastily as Joshua's scowl grew to dangerous proportions.

"The Scamp must have an accomplice in London," he replied coolly. "Or perhaps Johnnie himself operates out of the city. We never had any proof he's staying in our neighborhood."

Esther pondered this idea, unhappy to have her theories come to nought. It had been worrisome thinking the Scamp was staying at her inn, but it had been exciting, too. "You're probably right," she admitted. "Why must you always put a damper on any little excitement that comes along, Josh?"

"Murder and robbery are hardly the proper excitements for a young lady. You ought to be attending balls and parties."

She gave him an ironical glance. "I never miss the local assembly—two thrilling excitements a year. How do I stand the pace?"

Joshua studied her a moment. He told himself he disliked that strain of unsteadiness in Esther that must always have some rig running, yet it attracted him, too. To see her saucy shoulders slumped in ennui saddened him. To cheer her he said, "I hope you don't plan to miss my ball. I've decided to resume the tradition."

Her face lit up like a lamp. "Joshua! How splendid! When? Is it going to be very grand?"

"It will take a couple of weeks to prepare. We'll make it as grand as you like. Pick a theme—a masquerade party, perhaps."

"A formal ball! Lovely. I haven't had an excuse to buy a new ball gown in ages."

"Or a masquerade. Have you ever attended one?"

"No, but—"

"Then we must make it a masquerade, just for you."

Esther rather preferred a formal ball, but was pleased at the attention of having any sort of party in her honor, and didn't demur. "I'll help. I can write the cards for you."

"What will you come as, Esther? Pierrette? Cinderella?"

"I fancy myself as a more modern, enlightened lady."

"Madame de Staël, perhaps?" he joked.

"Or a working lady—say a publican."

He quelled his annoyance and smiled. "Would you like me to accompany you home now?"

"Oh, I am at home. I've moved into the inn," she teased.

"Esther!"

"Only for the nonce, while my house is being painted."

"You did it on purpose! You just wanted to be at the hub of all the excitement."

"Who would not?" She laughed. "Now it is beginning to seem all the excitement is over."

"You'd never know it to see the crowds in your lobby."

"And the Bow Street runners here, annoying my customers."

"Bow Street is here? I'll have a word with them."

Joshua left, and Esther went to sit in Buck's chair to think about the masquerade party. Now, what had made Josh decide to have it? Had he done it for her? She was interrupted by a tap at the door, and before she answered, Lady Gloria came tripping in, dragging an assortment of gossamer shawls after her. Her vague smile didn't deceive

97

Esther as to the reason for the visit. Lady Gloria always had a complaint. On this occasion she had more interesting words as well.

"Ah, Esther, I was expecting to see Buck, but you will do equally well. I'm afraid the strawberries were a leet-tle sour this morning. They weren't quite ripe, I think. I hope your guests aren't all suffering from the gripe as I shall be."

"I'll speak to Cook."

She hoped this would get Lady Gloria out the door, but the dame sat down and tilted her head conspiratorially toward the desk. In the sunlight her scalp showed through her thinning hair. "Quite a ruckus here today."

"Yes, we're rather busy."

"I was just wondering, Esther, whether I should mention Mr. Meecham to Bow Street."

"If Officer Clifford speaks to you, you might just mention the ladder incident."

"I had forgotten all about it. No, what I had in mind was the other . . . You haven't had any complaints about theft in your inn?"

Esther blanched. "What do you mean? Are you missing something?"

"Not I. You know I keep all my valuables about me." She patted the omnipresent pearls. "I referred to Mr. Fletcher. I saw Mr. Meecham slipping into his room last night, when poor Mr. Fletcher was asleep. It must have been two o'clock. I was awake. I have great trouble sleeping, but I don't say it is only the traffic in your halls that causes it. It is my age. So annoying, and I can't read as I used to, either. The eyes are gone."

"Lady Gloria, please continue. You saw Mr. Meecham enter Mr. Fletcher's room."

"I got up when I heard Meecham's door open. I

just opened my door a crack and saw Meecham slip in. He used a key to open the door—very odd, is it not? Well, as he had a key, I thought perhaps Fletcher had sent him to fetch something or other, and said nothing. Meecham was only in there for a minute—less! He came flying out and went to his room. He didn't seem to be carrying anything, but I did wonder if he had picked up Mr. Fletcher's money purse."

"Good God! You should have reported it!"

Lady Gloria was pleased with the excitement she had caused. Her visits were not usually received with such enthusiasm. "I told Buck this morning. He said he would speak to you, but with all the commotion . . ."

"Did Mr. Meecham leave his room again?"

"No, I kept a watch. He didn't leave."

"Was he sober? I mean did he stagger or anything?"

"Oh, sober as a judge. He was in his sock feet, and went slipping in ever so carefully. Certainly not disguised."

"I see." Esther was on thorns to be rid of Lady Gloria and follow up this new development. She rose and helped her guest from her chair, thanking her effusively and urging her to keep her eyes open for any other developments.

"Perhaps I should just mention one other little thing. It cannot be important, but—"

Esther pounced on it like a lion on a lamb. "What?"

"It's about the attics, dear. Mr. Meecham was up there yesterday afternoon. I happened to spot him slipping out. I'm afraid I don't know how long he was up there, or whether he hid anything up-

stairs. I only saw him come out, surreptitiously."
She nodded her head importantly on the last word.

"Out of the attics?"

"Yes. He was not inebriated, nor was he in his
stocking feet on that occasion. I shouldn't think
you need worry, Esther. There would not be anything worth stealing in your attics."

It was the possibility that Meecham was concealing stolen goods that disturbed Esther, and as
soon as she got rid of Lady Gloria, she scooted up
to the attics. He hadn't been foxed last night at
all. Why pretend he was? Her former trip with Mr.
Fletcher made it impossible to figure out where
Meecham had walked. The layer of dust on the
floor was so marked with their footprints that
Meecham's couldn't be distinguished. Why had he
gone to her attics? It could only be to hide something, perhaps the items stolen from the Higginses? His visit occurred before the gold robbery.

Esther spent the next hour searching through
trunks and in drawers of discarded lumber. There
were racks of old abandoned clothes offering good
concealment. It would be nearly impossible to find
a bit of hidden jewelry. She made a thorough
search and found nothing but was by no means
convinced that the goods weren't there.

When she returned to her room, an inn servant
was unpacking her trunks. "I thought you would
be finished long ago," Esther scolded.

"I won't be a minute, ma'am. Peters served us
tea in the kitchen, and some funny French sweets
he's trying for your inn, only they didn't turn out
right. They were so chewy, I nearly yanked a tooth
loose."

"I hope he doesn't plan to serve them to my customers."

"Oh, no, ma'am. Mr. Meecham—he was carrying down your tea tray—he tried one and said you wouldn't approve. He's ever so handsome, and jolly, too. Not toplofty like some gents."

"I expect he's left the kitchen by now?"

"Oh, yes. Peters took him down to show him the wine cellar, but he left ages ago."

Esther's face froze in annoyance. "I see."

She went to the window and looked out at the stable yard while her servant finished putting her things away. So Meecham had toured the cellars as well as the attics, had he? Perhaps he had better luck finding a hiding place there. He'd have a hard time getting to it, for the only routes were through the kitchen and Buck's office. Of course both these rooms were unoccupied in the middle of the night, when Captain Johnnie did his work. She'd warn Peters and Buck to lock their doors—not that a locked door was any impediment to Meecham!

She was of half a mind to enlist Fletcher's help. Certainly he should be notified that Meecham had entered his room while he slept. The nagging thought kept recurring that Meecham and Fletcher might both be involved in the robberies, and she had a strong aversion to their laughing at her behind her back. The fleeting visit might have been a midnight rendezvous to compare notes—or to plan the gold robbery. The proper man to speak to was Officer Clifford, and when her servant left, she asked her to send Mr. Clifford up.

Within minutes the sharp, twinkling brown eyes of Clifford were staring a question at her. She emptied her budget of Lady Gloria's news and her own. "What should we do?" she demanded.

"Nothing," he said bluntly. "Both Meecham and Fletcher have been here a few days. There's no way they could have known about the gold shipment. Those lads in London keep a close guard on when the wagon is to move out. It wasn't decided till a few hours before. There was no late-night rendezvous. What you have got on your hands is a simple thief, Miss Lowden. Meecham wants watching, but it's petty pilfering he has in his eye. Pretending to be foxed is an old con's trick. Your local constable can handle that. We're busy with bigger game. When Meecham saw Fletcher asleep, he left without risking a theft—or so I gather, as Fletcher hasn't reported anything missing. You might keep an armed man up to watch your safe at night. That's what your Meecham is after, I warrant."

"How reassuring! And why does he tour my attics and cellars, if it's the safe in my manager's office he's after?"

"That sort will take anything that's not nailed down."

"I thought you had a higher opinion of officers?"

"Some of 'em go bad. Pick up the looting habit abroad. 'Tis a pity. He might have thought to find a valuable antique in the attics and slide a bottle of wine under his jacket while he was belowstairs. Speak to the constable. You're in business, and must take a businessman's chances and precautions, and the thieves must deal with constables."

"Can't you take Meecham into custody?"

"I can only ask Mr. Fletcher to check if anything is missing from his room. If not—" He hunched his shoulders.

"Let me know what he says."

"That I will." Clifford left and was soon bobbing back. "Not a thing was missing, but Fletcher was

102

pretty upset that someone has a key to his room. He wants the lock changed."

"No one has a key to his room! Meecham must have a passe-partout. Surely that is enough to incriminate him."

"Not quite. It isn't against the law to own one, only to use it for unlawful ends, and as he didn't take anything, you have pretty slender evidence for starting a case against him."

Esther was dissatisfied with Officer Clifford. Meecham didn't strike her as a petty thief who would be satisfied with a couple of bottles of wine. She cudgeled her brains to involve Meecham in the affairs of Captain Johnnie and found it far from impossible. Last night he pretended to be foxed, but was, in fact, up and about at two o'clock in the morning, perfectly sober. He'd have had time to get to the heath and intercept the gold shipment—but he needed a colleague.

Fletcher? According to Lady Gloria, neither gentleman left his room, but even without a ladder, they could have reached the ground. A rope or knotted sheets would do the trick. And they could have got back in the same way. She must search their rooms, but first she must learn when they would not be in them.

It was lunchtime, and that was a good opportunity to learn how they planned to spend the afternoon. She didn't even have to ask Beau Fletcher. He came, smiling, up to her table, holding a letter.

"Great news, Miss Lowden." In front of her aunt he reverted to the more formal address. "I have just had a letter from Cathy. She is coming to join me for a visit."

"That is good news, Mr. Fletcher. How soon may we expect to see her?"

"I am going to London to pick her up today. I have been begging her to join me forever, and now she is with cousins in London. I plan to kidnap her and carry her home to the Lowden Arms."

"Won't you join us for lunch?" Esther said, and without further ado he drew out a chair.

Lady Gloria stopped on route to her table. "Why do you not join Lady Gloria, Auntie?" Esther suggested.

"She wants to be alone with her beau," Lady Gloria said waggishly.

It was exactly what Lady Brown feared, but she wanted a good cose with Lady Gloria and went along, leaving Esther and Fletcher alone. Beau immediately said, "You heard about last night? Meecham was in my room."

"Yes, I heard. I am terribly sorry, but I assure you Meecham doesn't have a key. You would hardly be safer if I changed the lock. Perhaps you should take Cathy to another inn," she suggested reluctantly.

"She'll have her woman with her, so she should be safe. I particularly want you and Cathy to meet. You know why I asked her here?"

Esther felt a warmth flush her throat and cheeks. Something in Beau's look caused it. He spoke on, "If I buy the inn, it will be her new home. I want her to come and see if she would be happy here."

"She would actually live at the inn?"

"Not exactly. I would turn a suite into an apartment for her. It is hardly worth buying a house, as she will be marrying soon and would rather have the cash for her dowry. Not that she is engaged, but she is at that age and is so pretty, she'll have a dozen offers."

"You are a very generous brother, Beau!"

"She's like a daughter to me. I confess I am very fond of her."

This didn't sound like a murdering highwayman. Esther found herself revising her thoughts. It was Meecham who was her main suspect now.

When they were finished, Fletcher accompanied her into the lobby. Meecham and Joshua Ramsay stood together, talking. Joshua scowled when he saw Esther with Fletcher. Meecham smiled blandly, unfazed that the whole inn knew he had sneaked into Fletcher's room the night before.

Esther burned with indignation at his impudence. How long must she go on harboring a thief? If she didn't set a trap, he might squat here for weeks. Very well then, she *would* set him a trap and bait it well. She walked forward purposefully, but was too discreet to reveal her plot immediately. It must seem to slip out naturally.

"Mr. Meecham, you are late dining today."

He bowed formally. "Miss Lowden, Fletcher."

"Are we to have the honor of your custom today, Joshua?" she asked.

"We were just discussing where to eat."

"You won't do better than my table. The excitement seems to be dying down, thank goodness. I wonder if Clifford has left." She allowed a worried frown to pucker her brow.

"I believe he's with Buck," Joshua said.

"Oh, good. I must speak to him. I am a little worried about the Wrothams. We had a note from Lord and Lady Wrotham, reserving a suite for the night. They are coming from London to attend their daughter's wedding in Farnborough. I expect they'll be carrying jewelry, and perhaps cash as well. I wish they were not arriving so late—ten o'clock. That will put them on the heath after dark, but Lord Wrotham probably has some cabinet business that detains him."

Joshua scowled, Meecham looked wary, and Beau Fletcher listened with no particular interest. "What do you expect Clifford to do?" Joshua asked.

"He could alert the guards on the heath. Not that they did much to help the men carrying gold last night," she replied.

"Anyone who ventures onto Hounslow after dark deserves what he gets," Meecham said rather angrily.

Fletcher gave him a blighting stare. "Spoken like a true Christian, Meecham." Then he took his leave.

"You shouldn't have mentioned the Wrothams' visit in front of Fletcher," Joshua scolded.

Esther didn't look within a right angle of Meecham. "Why not? You cannot think Mr. Fletcher would harm them?"

"I don't know what to think," Joshua admitted. "Meecham has just told me Fletcher was out of his room last night when the gold wagon was held up."

Esther turned a sapient eye on Meecham. "And how did you learn that, Mr. Meecham?" Could it possibly be true?

"I looked."

"Why?"

"Paul is keeping an eye on Fletcher for me," Joshua said.

"Again, might I know why? Why do you pick on him?"

"Because he's here."

Esther glanced innocently at Meecham. "So are

all my guests, Joshua. Surely that is not sufficient reason to condemn the man."

"I'm not condemning him. I'm just keeping an eye on him."

She felt a strong urge to mention the wisdom of keeping an eye on Meecham as well but didn't want to alert him that she had prepared a trap in inventing the Wrothams' visit.

"I'll let you two have your lunch now," she said pleasantly, and went to Buck's office to warn him he must corroborate the Wrothams' imaginary visit.

There were several important matters to arrange regarding her trap, but examining Meecham's room must be done first, while he was in the dining room. She had the master key and went along to his room quietly, to avoid detection by Lady Gloria or any other guests. The key turned in the lock, but the door refused to budge. He had barricaded it somehow from the inside. How had he done it? Was there someone in there? Had he pushed a dresser in front of it and climbed out the window? Esther was stymied.

As she passed Lady Gloria's door on the way to her own room, it occurred to her that she could reach Meecham's room by the interconnecting door from Lady Gloria's. These chambers used to be her mother's bedroom and sitting room. The door between was kept locked unless a family hired the two rooms as a suite. Lady Gloria might sit below with Lady Brown for an hour yet, gossiping over the teacups. Without a moment's hesitation she opened Lady Gloria's door and whisked inside, thence on to Meecham's room.

Mr. Meecham hadn't bothered moving any furniture behind his door into the hall. He had just jammed a knife into the molding around the frame that stopped the door from opening inward very effectively, though it did considerable damage to the molding and some to the knife.

She made a quick survey of the room. The window was open, which suggested Meecham had made his exit that way, in which case there should be a rope left hanging outside . . . but there was none. She stuck her head out the window and examined the side of the house for means of exit and reentry. Her eyes fell on the quoins at the corner of the building. They protruded two inches. A very agile man could clamber up them and reach the edge of the windowsill. The precaution of the knife in the door frame told her there was something worth concealing in the room and she set about finding it. Every place she looked held another piece of incriminating evidence. From the pistol under his pillow to the black mask and domino folded into a neat roll on the top shelf of his clothespress, to the long rope under his bed, everything shouted the same message: Captain Johnnie!

With her heart pounding in her throat, Esther quietly left and locked the door, then slipped out by Lady Gloria's room, locking it, too. Her fingers were trembling, and her knees felt wobbly. She went haring off to find Officer Clifford. Buck was in his office, paring his nails.

"Oh, hullo, Esther. I slipped over to the dower house. Pink. That dashed painter is doing you up in bright pink. I gave him a hand remixing till I got it toned down to a light rose blush."

"Thank you, Buck," she said distractedly.

"Is everything going all right?"

"Where's Officer Clifford?"

"He rode off not fifteen minutes ago. Said he'd be back around dinnertime. Bit of a relief to get his common phiz off the premises, what?"

"No, I need him. Where did he go?"

"He didn't say. Can I help, Esther?"

"I've found Captain Johnnie. It's Paul Meecham."

"Eh?"

"In his room—a gun, the black mask and cape, a rope—everything."

"Good God! I didn't see any of that when I searched earlier. Mind you, the grease spill on the carpet distracted me." Buck turned pale.

"He's with Joshua in the dining room now," Esther said.

"No, they went along to Heath Abbey. They decided not to eat here."

"Send Clifford to me the instant he arrives. And make sure your office is locked when you leave, Buck, and tell Peters to lock the cellar door in the kitchen as well. Meecham has been inspecting the whole place for hiding places for his loot."

"Eh?"

She repeated her morning's adventures. Buck was as nervous as a lady, which made Esther realize he would be no help in springing her trap. She'd leave that to Mr. Clifford.

She went upstairs, her head reeling with schemes, suspicions, and worries. Foremost in her mind was Joshua's troublesome report that Fletcher had not been in his room when Meecham entered. Where had he been? If his errand had been innocent, he would have told her. He had not seemed perturbed to hear of Meecham's visit while he slept, but Clifford had spoken to him first, so he was prepared. She must discover his first reaction, when Clifford told him. Why didn't Clifford come?

Chapter Nine

Esther saw from her window that Lady Brown and Lady Gloria Devere were taking a turn along the river walk and was relieved at their absence. Lady Brown would not approve of such unladylike doings as setting a trap for a highwayman and consorting with a Bow Street runner to do it. Yet something must be done to catch the Royal Scamp before he ruined her. Within an hour there was a tap at her door and Officer Clifford came in, eyes twinkling with curiosity.

"G'day, miss. Ye were looking for me?"

"Come in," she said, and hastily closed the door. When they were seated, she turned an accusing eye on him. "Why did you not tell me Mr. Fletcher was out of his room when Meecham sneaked in last night?"

"So that is what's got your dander up. The fact is, ma'am, Mr. Fletcher particularly asked me not to tell ye. He closed one eye and nodded sagely. "But as you've ferreted it out, 'twas petticoat dealings. I have just been having it checked out, and it verifies. A pretty little wench over at the Black Knight. He visited her last night and was there all through the robbery. He left the wench at five in the morning, to get back in his room before he was missed—except that Meecham slipped in around two and saw he was missing."

"A lightskirt!" Esther exclaimed. This was nearly as bad as robbing a coach. Worse, in that it lacked any daring and revealed only a dissolute side to the man. Any tinge of glamour Captain Johnnie's reputation had bestowed on Fletcher was quickly rubbed off, and he stood revealed in his true colors. "Well, upon my word!"

"Nothing to ruffle your fine feathers, milady. They all do it, and worse. And now I've a bone to pick with ye! Ye ought not to have announced in public that Lord and Lady Wrotham are coming to you tonight."

In her pique Esther had forgotten the more important reason for calling Clifford. She quickly outlined her plan. Clifford was not happy with her.

"Leave the catching of thieves to us that is trained for it," he said curtly. "What you have done is put me to a deal of bother for nothing."

"But if Meecham goes after the imaginary coach, it is an excellent opportunity to catch him."

"Catch him sitting on a horse in the shadows, minding his own business. You can't arrest a man for taking a moonlight ride, and that is all he'd be doing."

"If he goes to the heath tonight, we'll know he is Captain Johnnie at least. He has the pistol, the cape, and mask."

"I discussed them items with him when I spotted them in his room myself. Many gentlemen carry a pistol when traveling. He was at a masquerade party last week and kept the things, as it seems Joshua Ramsay is having another masked party."

"Mr. Ramsay only decided that this morning."

"Nay, 'twas decided before. Ramsay told me so hisself."

Esther found another slight in this. The party was not for her. It was Meecham who wanted a masquerade party. It had not been her first choice. "How about the open window and the quoins used as a ladder?"

"Meecham didn't build the quoins into the house. They've been there forever."

"He chose the corner room and left his window open."

"A body needs a breath of fresh air. Mr. Meecham is a gentleman of the first stare, Miss Lowden."

"You called him a petty thief before!"

"Aye, before I knew Mr. Joshua Ramsay had asked him in particular to look in on Fletcher's room. Everyone in London knows 'im, according to Mr. Joshua Ramsay. Meecham is kin to half the lords and ladies whose names pepper the journals for their social gadding. There's no way such a lad would risk his reputation. With his Adonis face he has only to marry an heiress, and any money troubles he has would be over with. It seems all the ladies are tossing their bonnets at his head. Ye don't go accusing someone like that, and a veteran besides."

Esther saw that Meecham was securely restored to his pedestal. "Why does he have that rope in his room, and why does he wedge his door with a knife?"

"He mentioned your poor fire-safety measures. Plenty of folks travel with a rope, in case of fire. Being near the back stairs, he figures he's in the worst location. A fire could come ripping up them stairs from the kitchen and burn you all to cinders.

113

It ain't my own area of expertise, but you ought to put in a set of fire stairs outside, miss."

"Why did he use a ladder the first night instead of coming in the door like a Christian?"

"I daresay he had wedged his door with a knife against thieves. The ladder was lying about handy when he returned, so he used it to crawl in. What ye didn't think to ask, miss, is how young Fletcher got in and out last night with no one being any the wiser."

"Rope or ladder?" she asked through thin lips.

"Rope. In his case it was your own good opinion he was fearful of losing, so he availed hisself of a rope and crept out and in that way."

"Does Meecham feel a knife stuck in his door would help his escape by a rope through the window, in case of fire?" she demanded.

"We all know public inns are beehives of thieves. He was only securing his valuables."

"He didn't have any valuables. He had a rope and a mask and cape."

"And a few odd bits of personal adornment ye missed. He keeps them in an empty wine bottle. A diamond stud, gold watch fobs, and whatnot. He showed them to me. A right clever lad, thinking of such a hiding place."

"Perhaps more clever than you know, Mr. Clifford. He's conned you."

"No, he gave reasonable answers to my questions, but that ain't to say I take his word for gospel. I'll keep an eye on him."

"And you'll follow him if he leaves the inn to intercept the Wrothams?"

"I will. Just in case he's connected with the Scamp, I want to learn where he stables his mount. He must have headquarters somewhere nearby.

Captain Johnnie must have, I mean, since we smoked him out of the Black Knight. That was his headquarters till a week ago."

Still miffed at Mr. Fletcher's duplicity, Esther said, "Perhaps Mr. Fletcher's wench could help you."

"She can't. She only moved into the Black Knight four days ago from London. Fletcher stayed there the night before he came here, and that is when he met her. A comely young girl."

Perhaps he would stop and visit the girl on his way to London to fetch Cathy. Esther felt her heart congeal to lava. She was furious with Fletcher for deceiving her, with Officer Clifford for not believing Meecham was guilty, and with Joshua for implying the masquerade party was for her. Most of all she was frustrated with not being able to do anything about the situation.

"What will you do tonight?" she asked sharply.

"I'll loiter about the inn, see who leaves, and follow him."

The afternoon seemed long. Beau was in London, and Joshua and Meecham didn't return from Heath Abbey. She had no idea what they were doing, or even whether they would return to the inn that evening. Meecham might go straight from the Abbey to his headquarters to saddle up and try to rob the Wrothams. Except that his mask and domino were presumably still in his room. Or would he have another set at his headquarters? At least he wasn't using her abandoned stable. A footboy from the inn had checked it out regularly, and no one had been there.

She felt a twinge of annoyance every time she thought of how her hospitality was being abused. She longed to throw Paul Meecham into the road like the thief he was, but with Joshua making a pet of him and Clifford singing his praises, she didn't dare to do it.

Dinner was an upsetting meal. Meecham had not returned, nor had she seen any sign of Joshua. Officer Clifford sat in a dark corner alone, shoveling in his mutton. Lady Brown babbled on in her usual aimless fashion. "We should take a run over to the dower house and see how the painting is going, Esther. I'm not sure you were wise to choose pink for the saloon. It can be gaudy, though it is flattering to aging complexions."

"Buck is keeping an eye on that, Auntie."

"I was looking forward to this stay at your inn, but now we are here, I find I miss the comforts of home. One doesn't like to go to her bedchamber at seven-thirty at night, nor to lounge about the lobby here like a commoner. Lady Gloria says the same. She has had a conciliating letter from her brother. He invited her back to the Hall. Of course it is only her fortune he is after, now that she is getting on in years, but I feel she will accept. No one wants to grow old alone, amid strangers."

This depressing talk did nothing to lighten Esther's mood. Was it to be her lot in life to grow old alone, at the inn? "At least Lady Gloria will have you for company this evening, Auntie."

"Yes, we will be playing cards in her room. You are more than welcome to join us."

To avoid this fate Esther said, "I have some business to discuss with Buck."

"Make sure he keeps the office door closed. You wouldn't want strangers staring in at you."

Eventually Lady Brown went upstairs to play cards with Lady Gloria, and Esther went to Buck's office, as it gave better access to Officer Clifford and doings at the inn. At eight-thirty Clifford came tapping at the door.

"No sign of Meecham," he informed Esther. "I daresay, he is still with Mr. Ramsay at the Abbey."

"Why don't you ride over and make sure?" she suggested.

"Nay, I have to keep an eye on the rest of your customers. Ye have other gents here that might be planning to strike out at nine to meet the Wrothams."

Esther looked at Buck. "Perhaps you would just post over to Josh's place, Buck. Ask him if he has the list for his ball ready. I have offered to write up his cards for him."

Buck's eyes grew wide. "You mean—go alone?" he asked.

Another hero. "No, go in the carriage, and take a groom with you."

Buck wiped his brow, where a film of moisture had sprung up. "I don't suppose Captain Johnnie would be working the main road, so close to town," he said, to ease his own worries.

"I shouldn't think so," Esther agreed.

Clifford listened. The lad had no more backbone than a dormouse. "Not a chance in Hades," he added. "He sticks to the heath, does Captain Johnnie."

Thus assured, Buck removed his watch, ring, and tiepin, just in case, and went to call the groom. Officer Clifford became bored with his vigil, and when two male clients left the dining room, he said, "That pair bears watching. I'll just follow them a ways down the road and see they don't veer off to the heath. There is no saying who might be the Scamp. I'd look nohow if I let him walk right out from under my nose."

Esther glanced out to see whom he had chosen for his quarry. "Why, that is Mr. Belfoi and his son. They stop for dinner every week on their way home from London on business. They will only be going home."

"In London every week, you say? That sounds highly suspicious."

"They'll take the west road home to Henley. They always do."

Clifford's eyes narrowed to slits. "So they'd have ye believe. I don't suppose you've ever followed them?"

"No, I haven't."

Clifford shook his head at her simplicity. He jammed on his hat and hustled out after the Belfois. Esther sat on alone. She did not feel it necessary to have the local judge and vicar followed when they left her dining room, nor did she think it likely a local family with two children would take to the heath. She drummed her fingers impatiently, occasionally glancing at the London newspaper that had arrived late that afternoon.

Half an hour later Buck returned unscathed. "Joshua wasn't home, nor was Meecham at the Abbey," he reported. They dined there early, but had left an hour before I arrived. Since Meecham left with Joshua, I shouldn't think you have to worry, Esther."

"Did you find out where they went?"

"They didn't leave word. Josh is probably taking Meecham to call on some of his relatives. He seems taken with the lad. Unlike Joshua to make a chum of a stranger on such short acquaintance," he mused.

"Then I guess there's nothing to do but wait. My little scheme has come to nought." She picked up the journal and began scanning the columns. Her eyes riveted on the report of Captain Johnnie's latest escapade, the holdup of the gold wagon. It gave an account of the guards who were murdered, the amount of gold coin taken, the intended destination, and so on. Toward the end she read, "Sir Clarence Fulbright, the deputy minister in charge of the transfer, is at a loss to know how Captain Johnnie learned of the shipment and believes he did not know in advance but came across it by accident."

Sir Clarence Fulbright! The very gentleman Joshua had spoken to in London. Joshua's main purpose in going to London was to hound Bow Street into a closer patrol of the heath. It must have been in his mind when he spoke to Fulbright. It was entirely possible Fulbright had mentioned the shipment leaving that very evening. But Joshua had denied it vigorously, as he vigorously denied that Meecham could possibly be involved.

Everything pointed to Meecham. Why would no one listen to her? She felt a rising panic and a growing certainty that Meecham was even now donning his black cape and mask—except that he was, presumably, with Joshua. Maybe he had made some excuse to get away.

"Buck, look at this," she said, fingering the article.

"I read it," he replied.

She told him about Joshua's conversation with Fulbright. "By Jove, you don't think old Joshua's tied up in this business!"

"Good Lord, no. That wasn't my meaning, but as he's so close with Meecham, he might have let something slip."

"Not if he didn't want to. Joshua's pretty close-lipped, and a clever rascal to boot."

Something in Buck's glinting eye sent a shiver up Esther's spine. Buck was suggesting that Joshua was personally involved in the doings of the Royal Scamp. It took her breath away to consider such a possibility. "What are you suggesting?" she asked. Her voice was high with disbelief.

"Joshua landed in just minutes before the Higginses the night they were robbed. You notice, he didn't stick around but left immediately. He was afraid they'd recognize him."

"That's true. I thought it odd, for he had promised to walk me home."

"There you are, then. And last night he and Meecham were whispering together in the card room. Minutes after, Meecham staggered upstairs playing at being foxed, but we know now he wasn't. Where did Joshua go? Did anyone ask him?"

"I didn't. But surely—oh, I can't believe it, Buck."

"He's powerfully set on picking up Pilchener's place. It costs a monkey, and how can he afford it?"

"But if this is true . . ."

"No real harm done. The Wrothams ain't coming. Don't I wish they were! Top of the trees. But they ain't, so you need not fear they'll be robbed."

"But I would like to discover if Meecham and—" she couldn't speak Joshua's name in such a context "—if Meecham is going after the Wrothams. I almost wish Beau Fletcher were here. He'd go after them fast enough." She looked at Buck assessingly.

He clutched at his cravat and backed away. "Now, Esther, don't say it. Don't even think it. I'm not riding out on the heath alone in the dead of night."

"You wouldn't be alone. You could take a footman—take two."

"*Send* two," he suggested, "as soon as Clifford returns."

"He should be here by now. He's probably following the Belfois all the way to the Henley turnoff. He'll be gone for an hour. We must do something, Buck."

"By 'we', you mean I must do something. This was all your idea. *You* go after them."

It was only desperation speaking, but Esther felt the justice of his claim. "I'll go with you. I'm not afraid."

"No! That would be worse than anything, to have a lady along to protect."

"You won't have to protect me. I'll carry a pistol. I know how to shoot. Papa's dueling pistols are in the safe. Get them out, and make sure they're loaded. I'll sneak down the kitchen stairs and meet you at the stable." She was already turning toward the door. "Send a set of footman's livery up to my room, Buck, and have our mounts saddled up. Oh, and have a footman occupy your office while you're away."

"Esther!"

She was already gone. Buck paced the office, scratching his head and muttering mild curses, but in the end his chivalrous instincts held sway, and he followed Esther's orders, to prevent the hurly-burly girl from going with only a footman to protect her. He should have bargained with her at least. This should have won him permission to hire a pastry chef.

While Esther snatched the blue livery from the servant and wiggled into trousers and jacket, Buck got out the pistols and carefully charged them. He held them as if they were red-hot, and might blow up in his face. When the distasteful job was done, he hid them under the newspaper, called in the head footman to guard his office, and went to the stable, where Esther was checking out Flame's reins. She had her hair stuffed up under a hat, the brim pulled low over her face to hide her identity. The bay mare snorted in pleasure at this unexpected outing.

"Have you got the pistols?" she asked.

"Under the paper," he muttered.

Mounting was difficult with his burden, but he finally got aloft and they cantered out to the road, where he gave Esther one pistol. His first concern was for propriety. "You're riding astride, Esther. You'd be ruined if anyone recognized you."

"No one did. I was careful."

"I must be mad to go along with this scheme. We should have brought a brace of footmen."

"It's only Joshua and Meecham."

"If we're right, it's only Captain Johnnie," he riposted, with heavy sarcasm.

"We're not going to do battle with them, Buck. We only plan to watch. If they're skulking on the heath, we'll know the truth."

"Small pleasure it will give me, I can tell you. I'll have to report that my cousin is a highwayman. By Jove, the disgrace will kill me if Josh don't. And then we'll have to stand in the box at Old Bailey and give evidence. I can't go through with it, Esther. Let us go home."

All this misery was every bit as distasteful to Esther as to her companion. "We'll do nothing of the sort. We'll tell Clifford, and he can catch them redhanded. He'll know then exactly whom to suspect and won't waste his time following the Belfois to Henley. He can set his own trap."

"If all we see is two dark forms skulking, how are we to know it's Joshua and Meecham?"

"We'll follow them at a discreet distance. If one sheers off to the Abbey and one to the inn, then we'll know."

After a short ride they came to the edge of the heath. Before them stretched the desolate waste dotted with low bushes and scrub, with an occasional tree casting a ghostly, mile-long shadow in the dim moonlight. The sickle moon far overhead looked white and cold and bathed the heath in silvery light. The heath was vacant of travelers, as far as the eye could see.

Buck exhaled a long sigh of relief. "They ain't here. Let us go home."

Esther spoke very reluctantly. "They wouldn't loiter this close to town. We have to ride a little way onto the heath."

"Josh and Meecham have gone somewhere to play whist. That's what it is. You can see there isn't a soul here."

"Then there's no danger. Come on." She dug her heels into Flame's flank and cantered ahead, with her heart racing in fear. Buck followed, most unwillingly.

As they rode, he kept up a nervous monologue that did much to destroy any shred of confidence left to her. "There's a small stand of trees and a hut a mile forward. If that's where they are, they could pick us off before we ever got a look at them."

"Be quiet, Buck. You're making my hair stand on end."

As they drew nearer to the stand of trees, their canter slowed to a walk. Every step was agony, as they wondered if a masked figure would dart from the trees, ordering them to stand and deliver. A slight breeze stirred the branches, causing a hundred false alarms. When Esther noticed Buck had taken his pistol from the saddle grip, she did likewise, but it was only scant help. They were highly visible. The concealing trees allowed no sign of their quarry. Esther swore a silent oath that if she escaped alive, she would never go in search of adventure again.

As Flame took the first step into the stand of trees, Esther feared her heart would burst. It pounded like a drum in her ears, muffling more important noises. Flame disliked the darkness, too, and whinnied her displeasure. It seemed a good excuse to speak, for Esther didn't think Joshua would actually shoot if he knew it was she. He would let her pass and hope she didn't discover him. "Good girl, Flame," she said loudly. Josh would recognize her mare's name. "Good Flame."

Buck sidled closer. His voice, when he spoke, trembled like a young girl's at meeting her beau. "I say, so far so good."

With white knuckles and bated breath, they passed through the dark spot and came out on the other side unharmed. Buck pulled to a halt. He gulped, and his body gave a convulsive shiver. "You may do as you like, Esther, but I ain't going another step. I wager my hair will be gray by the time we get home—if we get home alive."

Esther was greatly relieved at his stand. "Perhaps you're right. This is far enough. You can see another mile ahead, and there is no sign of life. We cannot ride all the way to London."

Yet, after so much trouble and danger, it was hard to go home no wiser than when they left. "Let us linger a while in the concealment of the trees," was her next suggestion. "If anyone comes, we are the ones who will have the advantage."

"I say we leave while we can."

"Just ten minutes, Buck."

He stared into the distance, gauging it impossible for anyone to reach the trees so soon. "Well, ten minutes, but then we leave." He had left his watch behind but thought he could estimate ten minutes fairly accurately. Only four minutes had passed when two dark figures appeared on the horizon, pounding *ventre à terre* toward them.

"Let's go!" he whispered. "We can make the edge of town before they reach us."

It was a strong temptation, but Esther held firm. "No, we'll go in behind the trees and wait. They'll never see us."

Buck didn't want to try to outrun them alone, and went along with her. His consternation was great when the riders slowed down as they approached the trees. The men were hardly even cantering, and it seemed possible they meant to stop altogether, which posed wicked problems. Esther peered through the concealing branches and was sure she recognized one of the mounts. The leader was certainly Joshua's Arabian, Sheba. As he drew nearer, she recognized Joshua's form, and her heart turned to stone. She hardly glanced at the other figure, but the outline looked like Meecham. They did not stop but continued at a leisurely pace, talking nonchalantly as they went.

"All a hum," Meecham said. She recognized his voice at this close range and suspected he spoke of the Wrothams. "Do you suppose she did it on purpose to test me?"

Joshua laughed lightly. "God only knows. I wouldn't put it a pace past her."

"She knows I'm your friend. Surely she doesn't suspect *you*."

"I doubt it. She thinks me too tame for such derring-do."

"She can't know you very well!"

Meecham's laugh told Esther his opinion of her and of her opinion of Joshua's daring. It was true then, Joshua, the respectable, dignified owner of Heath Abbey, was Captain Johnnie. A highwayman, and he stood up to read the epistle in church of a Sunday. He lectured her for running an inn, while he murdered innocent men and robbed the government of ten thousand pounds, to say nothing of all his other victims. She knew she should be furious, but her major emotion was deep, incredulous sorrow. She felt as if she had learned her father was a cutthroat pirate and her mother a lady of pleasure. Her idol, though she often argued with him, was a fiend. Nothing made sense in the world. Her eyes stung, and she realized she was fighting back tears.

Joshua and Meecham continued on, out of the wooded patch and toward town. When they were beyond earshot, Buck spoke.

"We'd best get home and tell Clifford."

"Yes, we had best get on with it," she said dully. The trip that had begun as an exciting escapade had turned to tragedy, or something very much like it. They rode home in silence, each nursing unpleasant thoughts: Buck of the disgrace to his family, and Esther of Joshua's perfidy.

Perhaps this was why he hadn't offered for her. A wife would hamper his nighttime activities. Was he so ambitious that he'd risk his reputation, just to enlarge his land holdings? He was ideally situated to perform this masquerade. His abbey was close to the heath, and his stable held all manner of prime bloods. His reputation prevented anyone from looking in his direction after a robbery. No one thought to inquire where Mr. Ramsay had been. He often went to London, arriving home late at night. As she reviewed the past, it occurred to her that he had more than once reported the Royal Scamp's work when he stopped at her inn or at the dower house. He always spoke in a derogatory way, but that was mere window dressing.

Now he was stepping up his foul work. For the gold robbery he required a partner, and Mr. Meecham had obligingly appeared on the scene, his credentials supported by Joshua. She wondered why Meecham didn't stay at Heath Abbey. That would have been more convenient for them, surely. Why was he putting up at her inn? Bow Street was in the habit of snooping around the inns, the Black Knight and her own. Did Josh want an ear to the ground—was that it? It was also a good place to learn of people's traveling plans. Josh had mentioned it himself.

As they drew near to the Lowden Arms, Buck said, "Why don't you run in the kitchen door, and I'll stable Flame for you, Esther."

"Thank you. I'll go up by the back stairs." Her voice sounded fatigued.

"Will you come down to the office later? We must talk about this."

"Yes, I'll come. Don't tell Clifford anything till I get there, Buck."

"I didn't intend to."

They exchanged a questioning look, but said no more. The idea was tacitly afoot between them that they would keep Joshua's secret. He must be

stopped, of course, but perhaps they could frighten
him into it by threats, without publicly shaming
him.

Chapter Ten

Esther looked up and down the hall to make sure no one was watching before she darted from the staircase to her room. She unlocked the door and stepped into the chamber, breathing heavily from the night's exertion. From the window a shaft of pale moonlight illuminated the shadowy rectangles of canopied bed and desk and bureau. The lighter object against the other wall was the chaise longue. She stood a moment, catching her breath. There was an eerie feeling to the night. It clung about her, seeming to permeate the very room, the air she breathed. She almost felt as if she were being watched. As she walked toward the lamp by her bed, an arm shot out and grabbed her around the waist. A hand clamped her mouth, and she was pulled firmly against a man's strong chest.

Captain Johnnie! was the thought that popped into her mind. Other confused ideas were there as well, reeling about with the sheer terror of the moment. He never attacked women like this before. My God, who else in her inn had he molested? Was it Meecham, a petty thief as well as a highwayman? She waited, her whole body tensed, ready to defend, not yet thinking of attack.

The man spoke in a low, menacing voice. "Don't shout. Not a sound." Joshua! She twisted around to confirm that it was he. "Esther? My God, I thought you were a man! I thought you had slipped in to rob—" His hand fell from her mouth, lighting on her wrist. He loosened his grip around her waist, but did not release her. "What the devil are you doing in trousers?"

Shock and the aftermath of terror held her silent. From the circle of his arms she stared at his rugged face, each strong feature etched in the moonlight like charcoal on paper. His eyes were a sparkle of black diamond beneath his dark brows. His jaw was square and hard; his mouth, rigid in disapproval, looked cruel. She felt she had never known Joshua Ramsay. She was looking at a stranger, and a frisson trembled up her spine.

"Let me go," she said, but her words were nearly inaudible and went unheeded.

"So you *did* go to the heath," he said, in an accusing tone. "I trust you didn't go alone."

"B-Buck went with me."

"That man-milliner! You might have been killed."

"I was safe enough—till I entered my own bedchamber. What are you doing here?"

Joshua released her then. "When I saw your mount was missing from the stable, I was afraid you might have gone haring off to the heath. It was all a stunt, that Wrotham business, wasn't it?"

She backed away from him, rapidly planning how to handle the situation. "Yes, it was a ruse; I hoped to draw Captain Johnnie out."

An angry scowl creased his brow. "There's more

130

to a ruse than that. You should have had Bow Street out in force."

"I tried to enlist Clifford's help. He—oh, never mind." She tossed her head and strode away. Should she reveal her dreadful knowledge? Would Joshua harm her? It seemed unreal, almost a nightmare that she should fear for her physical safety with Joshua.

When he spoke, she sensed a new menace in him. "Where were you, exactly, on the heath? You can't have gone far. It must have been at the first stand of trees. You saw us. . . ." The words fell like quiet thunder.

Her first intention of confronting him faded away. She couldn't do it now, here, alone and isolated. She had planned to do it in Buck's office, with Buck present. "No!"

"Of course you did. Why the devil didn't you say something, let us know you were there?"

"I—I wasn't sure it was you. Was it Meecham with you?"

"Yes, we rode out, hoping to catch Captain Johnnie as he attacked the Wrothams."

Esther pondered this bland assertion. In the darkness, with fear still enshrouding her, and with the new feeling of danger and uncertainty that clung around Joshua, she found it hard to believe his story, but wise to pretend to. "I see," she said.

"We thought Fletcher's trip to London to fetch his sister might be a ruse. We hoped to catch him red-handed, but he didn't fall for your simple trap."

"Why don't you wait for me in Buck's office till I change, and we'll talk?"

"We can talk here; it's more private."

This impropriety was so unlike Joshua that a new spasm of fear gripped her. She edged toward

131

the bell cord by the chaise longue, to summon help from below if necessary. "What is there to talk about?"

"I know you're suspicious of Meecham," he said.

"Not without reason."

"I had a few doubts myself, when Clifford told me about that rope in his room and the business of putting a knife in his door, and so on. In fact, I decided to follow him tonight and invited him to dinner at the Abbey to make it easier. It was nonsense. He suggested himself that the pair of us go after Johnnie."

"He might have guessed that you suspected him. That would be a good way to divert your suspicions."

"That's true, but I've come to trust Paul. I wish you would do the same."

Esther hardly knew whether she even trusted Joshua, let alone Meecham. His story could be true, but it could also be a tale designed to fool her. "Meecham has the knack of disarming people's suspicions. Even Clifford believes him." She wandered to the chaise longue and sat on the very edge of it, ready to spring if necessary or pull the bell cord. Her nerves were tensed to painful wariness.

Joshua followed her. She feared he was going to crowd on beside her, but he just crouched on one knee at her feet, and took her two small hands in his. Was that to prevent her from pulling the cord? "Leave it alone, Esther," he urged. "This is no business for ladies. We'll catch Johnnie. You just prepare for my ball. I've had the list of guests drawn up. Perhaps you'd help my housekeeper arrange the details. Come over tomorrow morning, and we'll begin plans. I don't want anything to happen to you."

His voice was gentle now. He lifted her hand and drew it to his lips, where he placed a kiss on her palm. It was not the sort of romantic gesture she expected from him. He was a different man tonight. The Joshua she thought she knew would not go hounding after a highwayman. He would certainly not fall under suspicion of *being* Captain Johnnie. And her heart would not pound erratically at his touch. How contrary life was. She could love him when she thought him a menace. It was the dash of spice dull Joshua needed to make him interesting. But she could not in a million years marry a man who might be a highwayman.

"I'll let you get to bed now," he said, rising. Before he left, he smiled, rather rakishly. "I hope my behavior tonight hasn't given you a disgust of me. I'm not really in the habit of forcing my way into ladies' chambers."

"How did you get in? The door was locked."

"Paul let me in. He has a key that opens any door. The servants told me you were in your room, but you didn't answer when I knocked. If you weren't here, I had planned to mount a rescue party and go after you."

"Don't you find it suspicious that Paul has a passe partout?"

Joshua jerked to attention and hesitated a moment before replying. "They gave it to him at Whitehall. He has to have access to many rooms for records and so on."

"I see." She mentally congratulated him. Very good, Joshua. You came up with a defense of your cohort more quickly than I would have thought.

"Lock this door after me."

"Much good it will do!"

But she did lock the door and quickly scrambled out of trousers and into a gown to go below to visit Buck. Joshua had left the inn, and Meecham was nowhere about when she went into the lobby. When she entered Buck's office, he jumped to his feet. "I have just suffered a visit from Joshua," he announced. His face was pink with anger or frustration. "He came ringing a peal over me for subjecting you to danger."

"I had a word with himself myself," she said, but didn't go into any details. "I suppose he told you that Banbury tale about being on the heath to catch Captain Johnnie?"

"He explained why he and Meecham were there," Buck replied, and he apparently had swallowed the story whole. "We might have known it was something of the sort. I mean, Joshua Ramsay—he'd no more hold up a coach than I would. Less—he has plenty of blunt. I'm a younger son who must fend for himself."

Normally Esther would have agreed with him, but tonight Joshua had seemed different. "What do you think about Meecham? Perhaps he twigged to it that Joshua meant to follow him and knew he couldn't go after the Wrothams, so suggested to Joshua they go together, to defuse his suspicion. Joshua admitted he did suspect Meecham."

"I don't give a tinker's curse who Captain Johnnie is. Joshua ordered me to keep you from doing anything else rash. I mean to follow that order, Esther. If you plan to catch the Scamp, you must find yourself another partner. While we were away, that silly ass of a footman I left in charge turned two customers from the door. He thought we had no empty rooms, and half the top floor is empty. And here is a note from Peters. The mutton we planned to serve tomorrow didn't arrive. How are we to feed our hungry guests? Oh, and I meant to answer these notes from London. The rooms are filling up nicely for the boxing-match weekend in May."

Buck's mind was obviously on inn business, and as it was pointless to accuse Joshua of being the Royal Scamp to his naïve cousin, there was nothing else to discuss. But Esther wasn't convinced Joshua had been telling the truth.

As she left the office, she noticed Officer Clifford talking to Meecham. They went into the taproom, and she went upstairs to have a few words with her aunt and Lady Gloria before retiring. To please her aunt, she mentioned speaking to Joshua and helping him with the ball.

"We'll drive over to the Abbey tomorrow morning," her aunt said.

"Yes, Josh suggested it." And while she was there, she'd do a bit of snooping. If Joshua was the Royal Scamp, there might be some evidence at the Abbey. Just what that evidence might be she had no idea, but the wagonload of gold had to be somewhere. The whole wagon had been stolen, and the Abbey was the likeliest spot to hide it.

After breakfast the next morning Lady Brown suggested they call the carriage to go to the Abbey, but Esther wanted to get into Joshua's stables and declared she was dying for a ride. Her aunt drove; Esther rode beside her and took her own mount to the stable. She looked down the box stalls and counted three mounts dark enough to look black at night.

"I'll take care of Flame for you, Miss Lowden," the stableboy offered.

"Would you get her some water, please?"

As soon as the boy left, she ran the length of the stable, peering into corners for the wagon. There was no sign of it, and, of course, no piles of gold. How would it be packaged—in bags, in boxes? Perhaps the gold was in the hayloft? But the wagon certainly wasn't. It could be buried under any haystack on the estate, or even disassembled by now. The stableboy returned with the water, and Esther left the stable. As she went toward the Abbey, she noticed two of Joshua's laborers were tending a bonfire.

This wasn't unusual. There was always plenty of debris to be gotten rid of on a large estate, and what could be burned was. A wooden wagon, however, could also be disposed of in this manner without leaving a trace but the hardware. She sauntered over to the fire and peered into the flames. There was a large mound of cinders and ash below the fire. It must have been burning for hours. On top, the men were piling on house refuse: old journals and magazines, a dilapidated kitchen chair, and bags that once contained flour and sugar. The stench in the air suggested that food remains were below the dry fire fodder. And if the ashes of a government wagon were below it all, she had no way of knowing, but it seemed significant that Joshua was having the monthly bonfire at this precise time.

It was always a pleasure to enter the Abbey. Joshua's household was well run. On a fine morning in spring sunlight struggled through the vine-tangled windows of a small saloon, glinting off brass lamps and old carved furnishings. On the walls Dutch paintings glowed like jewels. Why Joshua chose to hide such lovely paintings in a small saloon was a mystery to Esther. The Vermeers were small but exquisitely done, a companion set of women working in the kitchen. Lady Brown was already established behind a desk with a list and a pile of white cards before her.

She lifted her head and said, "Joshua is waiting for you in the ballroom, Esther. He wants your suggestions for decoration." A hopeful smile lifted her lips. "A ruse to get you to himself," she said archly.

And an excuse for me to poke through a few more saloons, Esther silently added. She went into the hall, and when she found it empty, she drifted into his office, silently closing the door behind her. A massive oak desk occupied the center of the far wall. She hastened to it and looked through the papers on top. She glanced at bills for farm supplies and receipts from buyers of his produce. Nothing suspicious here. She slid open the top drawer and found herself staring at an offer to purchase Pilchener's estate at a price of ten thousand pounds. The sum was fresh in her mind, the exact amount stolen in the gold shipment. She silently closed the drawer and went to the ballroom, warning herself to hide her knowledge.

The man standing in the middle of the room gazing all around him with an air of quiet satisfaction looked like any prosperous country squire. His jacket, though well cut, did not aspire to city heights of fashion. His waistcoat was a discreet stripe, and the topboots he wore had no foppish white bands. It wasn't a desire to cut a dash in society that would lure Joshua into robbery, but would his lust for land do it?

"There you are." He smiled and paced forward to meet her. "I have just been imagining this room full of masked revelers. In May, I think simple baskets of flowers will give a festive touch. I'm glad you nagged me into having this ball, Esther."

But the ball had been arranged before he spoke to her, or what excuse did Mr. Meecham have for that domino and mask in his room? "Have you set on a date?"

"Yes, we're rushing it forward—next Friday night. That gives us ten days."

"Your invitations will hardly have time to be received and answered. Or will they be mostly local guests?"

"Not at all. I'm inviting some members of London society for the weekend," he said, and named half a dozen of the ton.

"I hope you warn them not to bring their jewels."

"Ladies won't appear in public without their gewgaws, but I am suggesting they form a caravan and all come together, with armed footmen. I don't expect they'll wait till dark to make the trek, either. I am suggesting they come in midafternoon. They'll stay the weekend and return in daylight on Monday. I hope you and your aunt will come over even earlier and play joint-hostesses for me."

"We'd be delighted to. You have given a deal of thought to your guests' safety." Of course Captain Johnnie would hardly rob his own guests, so that proved nothing.

"What do you think of my idea for floral decorations?"

"Not original, sir, but as you are rushing the thing forward as though it were a wedding of necessity, you don't leave me much time for improvement."

Joshua glanced down at her with a smile in his

dark eyes. "Next year, you can have it all your own way. Start thinking now, and devise any fantasy that suits you. You could do it in Persian tents à la Byron, or chinoiserie, in the royal fashion of Prinny—or in the 'horrid' style of Otranto's castle, with ghosts lurking in dark corners."

"Money is no object, I see," she said, and looked for his reaction.

"Sheets for ghosts don't cost much."

"It wasn't the Otranto theme that appealed to me, Josh. I rather like your suggestion of Persian tents."

"I daresay a few yards of muslin won't break me."

"More than a few yards. Why, at this rate, you won't be able to afford Pilchener's place," she said offhandedly.

Josh just smiled and said not a word about already having made an offer on it. "If there is anyone you would like to invite to my ball, just add your names to the list."

The name that occurred to her was Mr. Fletcher, but she had lost her enthusiasm for him. "I would like to ask Lady Gloria. She would enjoy it."

He peered playfully down at her. "No one else?"

"I'll think about it."

"You do that. Ask anyone you like; you have carte blanche. No need to check with me. I'm sure your discretion may be counted on not to lumber me with undesirables."

It almost seemed he was urging her to ask Fletcher, but she refused to recognize the hint. "If Officer Clifford is still about, it might be a good idea to have him here. He might pass for a gentleman in a domino if he keeps his mouth shut, and he can help you guard all the valuables that will be in the house."

"A good idea. I'll speak to him. Your aunt tells me you rode over this morning. I hope you had an escort."

"I accompanied her carriage."

"That's a slow, dragging ride. I'll send one of my men home with you, to allow you a good gallop."

Esther felt a spurt of annoyance that soon turned to suspicion. She had planned to check out his land and couldn't do it if Joshua's man accompanied her. Was that why he suggested it? "I'm not in the mood for a gallop today. I'll accompany Auntie's carriage home," she said.

He nodded in satisfaction. "I've had the servants haul baskets and vases into the morning parlor to save your going to the attics. Shall we have a look at them?"

"You must have other things to do, Josh. Just leave me to it."

He pulled out his watch. It was an old turnip timepiece inherited from his father. Joshua really did not indulge himself in toys. "I do want to speak to my banker this morning. I've notified the gardener you'll be speaking to him. I'll ask the servants to bring you and Lady Brown coffee in an hour."

"Thank you."

He left in very good spirits. At the doorway he turned and waved, with a musing smile on his usually dour face. He thought he had conned her, she assumed, and wondered why he had gone to the trouble of having baskets and vases brought down from the attics. Was it to keep her out of them? As soon as the door closed behind him, she went into the hall and up the front stairs. Esther was familiar with the Abbey and went directly to the attic door and up the staircase.

The air was close in the silent attics under the eaves. There were no lamps, but the windows gave plenty of light. She looked at the sprawling space and knew it would take a week to find anything Joshua had hidden there. There was no dust on the floors to leave guiding footsteps. Even his attics were kept clean. She wandered from room to room, opening trunks and peering into drawers of discarded chests, but found only ancient clothing and yellowing linen and bundled parcels of letters, with fading ink in spidery script. She looked around, wondering if there might be something to use for the ball, and found a rather pretty trellis arch that would make a suitable entrance to the ballroom with flowers and vines in the latticework.

She returned below and asked a servant to bring it to the ballroom, and went to the conservatory to speak to the gardener. They went into the garden to discuss what would be in bloom in ten days' time and what plants should be bought and hired. The gardens were lovely, stretching for hundreds of yards. Roses—red, pink, yellow, and white—nodded in the sun, with the blue sky arched above. Such a beautiful day, such a beautiful place—she resented having to think of catching a thief.

In an hour she joined her aunt for coffee and suggested they take the cards and list back to the inn for writing up. "I shan't be returning with you after all," she said, and felt badly about lying to her aunt. "Joshua offered me an escort home," she added. That at least was true; she didn't say she had refused the offer.

"So thoughtful. One cannot help but thinking,

141

when she is at this lovely abbey, how fine it would be to be mistress of the place."

The same thought had occurred to Esther. "Yes," she said, rather wistfully. "It does seem—spacious—after the dower house, does it not?" And the grounds, at least, would be even more spacious after Josh bought Pilchener's property.

Esther went to the stable and tarried till her aunt's carriage had left. Then she mounted Flame. The stableboy looked a question when she headed out alone. "Shall I go with you, Miss Lowden?" he asked.

"I'll catch up to the carriage," she said, and trotted Flame out toward the main road. But when she was beyond view of the house, she detoured into the park and thence through the fields. Men were cutting the first hay crop, so she couldn't check the haystacks for a concealed wagon, but she cantered through the spinney and woods, peering for signs of a wagon's passing. It would have left a trail through the undergrowth off the main path. She saw no such trail. It was peaceful in the woods, with the tall trees providing shade and scenting the air with resin. Wildflowers bloomed between the trees, carpeting the forest floor with patches of white and yellow and blue. Overhead, disturbed birds chirped their displeasure with her presence.

It was another fruitless effort—the estate was just too big for one person to search—and she went home. Lady Brown had arrived before her, unaware that she had made the trip alone. Lady Gloria was sipping tea in the morning parlor and beckoned Esther in.

"Have you heard?" she asked, her little gray head bobbing like a bird's, as she pulled her shawl around her narrow shoulders. "I've just been reading in the paper that they've found the wagon that held the gold. It was empty, of course."

Esther's heart was clenched like a fist. "Where?" she demanded.

"In the Thames River, not too far from London. It was driven into the river, but a boater came aground against it and saw the printing on the side. It was a government wagon, you know. The gold is in London by now. There is no hope of ever recovering it. They found one of the nags, too."

Esther felt her heart ease back to normal. "In London?" she asked.

"Yes. Johnnie has got away with another fortune. The man must be rich as Croesus. What a high life-style he must enjoy. A fine home and servants, and anything he likes to eat and drink. Quite like the old days at the castle. Oh, and speaking of food, Esther, you might just mention to your manager about breakfast. I found my eggs just a teensy bit hard this morning. I don't know how many times I have told them two minutes, but they will keep bringing them as hard as a rock, and an overcooked egg tastes like bile."

"I'll tell Buck right now," she said, and used it as an excuse to get away.

She went to Buck's office and tapped at the door. "Esther, come in. I have been thinking about this pastry business, and really we must hire a pastry chef."

"Later, Buck. Did you know your cousin has put an offer on Pilchener's place? For ten thousand pounds," she said, and directed a meaningful look at him.

"The devil, you say! Where is he getting the blunt?"

"That's a good question. Oh, incidentally, while

Lady Gloria was complaining about her hard eggs just now, she told me they have found the wagon that held the gold in the latest robbery. It was in the Thames. Ten thousand was taken, you remember?"

"I certainly do. Couldn't I use ten thousand! I have had another set-to with Papa. He stopped in for a minute to harangue me. Called me an inn maid, by the living jingo. I told him I had no thought of giving up my career. There will be nothing for me from Papa, I fear."

"He'll come around in time, Buck. Pilchener's place costs ten thousand," she said, to make her meaning perfectly clear.

"Don't narrow your eyes at me like that, Esther. Josh didn't steal it. I think I know my own cousin."

"I thought I knew him, too, but lately he seems— different."

"He seems as toplofty as ever to me. Your aunt was just telling me about his masquerade party. That is a little unlike him to be spending his money on frivolity. I daresay he has his eye on some London lady and is out to impress her."

"London lady? What do you mean?" she demanded.

"It stands to reason he must have in mind nabbing an heiress. Why else would he feel free to spend ten thousand pounds? The Chalmers chit, likely. She has a dot of twenty-five, I've heard him say."

Esther scowled and ran to check the invitation list for Miss Chalmers. Her mood was not improved upon finding Lord and Lady Chalmers and their daughter, Lady Margaret, at the top of the list. And he had said he was having this ball for her. She knew all along that wasn't the reason, but to have it confirmed stung like a nettle. Let him write his own invitations, the pest.

Chapter Eleven

Esther did write one of the invitations to Joshua's ball. It was addressed to Mr. Beau Fletcher and Miss Fletcher. Beau arrived back at the Lowden Arms that same afternoon, in time for dinner. Though she was still angry with him, and with the whole world, Esther decided he would make a good flirt to annoy Joshua, and wrote up the invitation before dinner. She was rather curious to meet Miss Fletcher, as Beau spoke often of her, always in the highest terms.

What he had never mentioned, and what came as a great disappointment, was that Cathy was invalidish. Beau had to carry her into the inn, swaddled in blankets. It was Lady Gloria Devere who told Esther about it at dinner that evening.

"She was overcome with heat, poor thing," Lady Gloria explained, "and it was only sixty-three degrees. I find the air quite chill. In fact, my room is freezing at night."

"You must ask the servants to lay a fire," Esther said.

"I have asked your manager a dozen times to have the grate cleaned. One hardly knows which is worse, the cold or the smoke."

"I'll speak to him myself," Esther said, and reverted to the more interesting subject. "What did Miss Fletcher look like, Lady Gloria? Is she pretty?"

"Even her face was covered. I hinted for an introduction as Mr. Fletcher carried her into the lobby, but he was rather brusque, I fear. Not exactly rude, you know, but curt. He said he had to get her to bed immediately. Perhaps it was the crowds in the lobby that deterred him. That Mr. Meecham was there, speaking to your manager and Officer Clifford, and some new patrons were just entering. They would all have crowded around, I daresay. He is a very considerate brother," she added, "unlike some."

Lady Brown recognized a hint in this that Lady Gloria's own brother was being selfish again, and the conversation turned to that well-worn topic. It seemed there were strings attached to Lady Gloria's invitation to return to the family mansion. The strand on which Lady Gloria expatiated for the remainder of dinner had to do with reroofing that portion of the house where her apartments were located. "He must take me for a naïve girl," she snorted. "Lead roofing costs a fortune."

Esther thought Cathy might be sufficiently recovered to come downstairs for dinner, but she was disappointed. Her brother ate with her in her room, but he met Esther later in the hall as she was going upstairs.

"Esther, nice to see you again. Did anything exciting happen during my absence?"

She examined him coolly. "The only exciting thing that has happened today is your sister's arrival. I hear she is indisposed. I hope it is not serious?"

"Cathy always suffers in a carriage. The doctor calls it motion sickness. I hope she will be better soon."

"I trust she is resting comfortably?" He nodded, and Esther continued, "When may we meet her?"

"Very soon. If she is not able to leave her room tomorrow, I'm sure she would be happy to receive you there. I shall have to spend a good deal of my time with her," he added. His smile suggested his presence would be the real treat.

To show her new state of pique, Esther said, "Just let me know when you want a respite, and I shall be happy to replace you."

Beau shuffled his feet, peered at her from the side of his eyes, and eventually said, "I expect Officer Clifford has been telling tales on me."

"Telling tales suggests a misrepresentation of the facts, Mr. Fletcher. If he is slandering you, I suggest you speak to him."

"No, what he said is true. I *was* at the Black Knight that evening, with—well, you know who I was with," he mumbled sheepishly.

"Whom you or any of my clients associate with away from my inn is no concern of mine, just so you don't bring your women here."

"Esther, I'm sorry. Can't we go somewhere to talk in private?"

"We are quite alone here," she pointed out.

"It is not very intimate. The fact is, it is deuced lonesome for a young chap away from home. I daresay being in the navy didn't help. One is considered less than a man if he hasn't a woman in every port—not that I mean to imply I had! I want to settle down. That is one of the reasons I was so eager to have my sister with me. Cathy will be company, someone to talk to in the evenings—till

I find a permanent companion." His speaking blue eyes gazed meaningfully into hers. Seeing only anger, he changed tack. "You still haven't given me a price on the inn."

Though she didn't reveal it, Esther was swayed by his long lashes and sincerity, and perhaps by a desire to sell her troublesome inn. Of course she was also in favor of reformation. "I'll have to discuss it with my manager. We should do an inventory, I suppose."

"We'll talk about it tomorrow. I'll be around all day, as Cathy is not well."

"Did her woman not come with her?"

"Miss Vaughan will be joining us shortly. She didn't feel up to the trip today. She's had a bout of flu, poor thing. I hope Cathy hasn't taken it."

"How tiresome for her."

"Yes, and she is elderly, too. It takes the oldsters a while to recover. I was just going to the lobby for a newspaper. Did Captain Johnnie play off any tricks while I was away?"

"We haven't heard of any."

"I thought that noble couple you mentioned—the Rotherhams, was it?—might have fallen victim. I assume they arrived safe and sound."

"The Wrothams didn't come after all. We received a cancelation in the afternoon," she added vaguely.

"I didn't like to say anything the other day, but it seemed ill-advised of you to mention their coming in such a public place."

"You're quite right. I'll be more careful another time."

Beau left to pick up the journals, and Esther went to her room. After fifteen minutes' pacing, she was sympathetic to Lady Gloria's views on living in an inn. She was bored to flinders in her room but disliked to loiter about the lobby or common room and had even less desire to play cards with the older ladies. She decided to discuss Fletcher's offer to buy with Buck, but when she entered his office, he wasn't there. The door leading to the wine cellars was ajar, and a dim light below told her someone was there.

Before there was time for an image of a masked highwayman to pop into her head, the reassuring echo of Buck's voice came up the stairs. "Five hogsheads of the best sherry, about a thousand bottles of claret and port, and, of course, our house wine. We buy that from Wilbert's in London. Would you like to try a glass?"

"Port's my drink," Mr. Fletcher's voice replied.

Their footsteps receded into the farther reaches of the cellar, and Esther sat down to wait. Beau certainly wasn't wasting any time beginning an inventory of her wine cellars. She picked a newspaper from Buck's desk and glanced at it. He had drawn lines around a few notes in the social columns. The DeHavens were going to a houseparty at Harrington Hall. Lord Mundy was expected to arrive in London with his daughter, who would be making her bows. Now why had Buck circled those items? Was it potential customers for her inn? Both would be passing the Lowden Arms, one from the east, one from the west. People were foolish to publish these announcements when the heath was so unsafe.

Esther knew a wine cellar was a place where bibulous gentlemen could happily spend an entire evening, and after a few moments she returned to her room with the newspaper. Her object was to read the estate advertisements and determine what price an establishment of her sort might hope to fetch on the market. She was pleasantly surprised to discover she was richer than she thought, or would be when and if she sold. It appeared that Mr. Fletcher, at least, was serious about buying.

He planned to continue running the establishment as an inn, and a part of the place's value was its goodwill. Meecham, on the other hand, planned to make it his home and would not be willing to pay for any intangible asset. But as Josh was buying Pilchener's, Meecham would presumably be staying there. His snooping had nothing to do with buying, but was only a stunt to familiarize himself with the various passages.

Inevitably she found herself thinking about Captain Johnnie—and Joshua—and Lady Margaret. When had this romance sprung up between them? Joshua often went to London on business. He might have been courting her for a year. The ball might be to announce their engagement, for all she knew. Anger stirred in her breast. As she sat, she mentally devised a costume for herself that would outdo Lady Margaret's and that of any other fine lady who had set her cap at Joshua. The ball had a May Day theme. She would attend as Queen of the May, with flowers twined in her hair, and wearing a flowing white gown. She sketched it, and planned to purchase her material the next day.

For a week things went on quietly enough at the inn. The first priority was the writing and dispatching of the invitations. The ladies were busy with their costumes. Officer Clifford continued to haunt the passages, stopping frequently to quiz Esther about some detail. Captain Johnnie did not strike, though several lesser minions of the moon

151

relieved passengers of their money and valuables. Mr. Meecham hung on, often visiting Joshua for a day at a time. Miss Fletcher turned out to have suffered more than motion sickness. The girl had come down with a bad case of Miss Vaughan's flu. Esther did not have to be hinted from the door. She had no wish to contract the ailment herself. Beau spent a good deal of time with Cathy, but it bothered Esther not a whit. She spent much time at Heath Abbey, consulting with the cook and housekeeper and gardener and Joshua about the ball.

As she was preparing to leave the Abbey one afternoon, Joshua met her in the garden. "I'm happy to see you've taken the reins of my ball, Esther," he said. "I'm not much good at this sort of thing."

"We want to impress Lady Margaret," she replied, with a teasing sparkle in her eye. His self-conscious look told her what she was eager to know. There was something between them. Esther damped down her vexation and said, "Will you be announcing your betrothal?"

"Betrothal! It hasn't gone that far."

"How far has it gone?"

"Preliminary investigations only. What made you think I was going to offer for Lady Margaret?"

"Buck suggested it."

Josh gave her a conning look. "I wonder why? Perhaps he dislikes your coming so often to visit me."

"Why would he? I'm not abandoning my duties at the inn."

"No, but you are abandoning him."

Esther stared in amazement. "Are you suggesting there is something afoot between Buck and myself?"

"You two spend a deal of time together. You seem to get on pretty well. Buck has his fortune to be made. Marrying an heiress is one way to set about it. You are not completely without dowry. The fact that it is tied up in an inn would not distress him. He seems quite at home there."

Laughter was the only possible reply to such an outré idea, and Esther laughed heartily. When she had stopped laughing, she said, "My funds may be freed sooner than you think. Mr. Fletcher is seriously interested in purchasing, unlike your Mr. Meecham. He hasn't approached me at all." And still, Joshua said not a word about purchasing Pilchener's place.

"What did Fletcher offer?"

"We haven't set a price. He spends considerable time with Buck, though, going over the inventory and so on."

"Have you met this mysterious sister, Cathy?"

"No, she has the flu."

"I hope she is recovered in time for the ball. You *did* invite Fletcher?"

"You gave me carte blanche. I asked him and his sister." She peered for his reaction, which was mildly approving. "She must be improving. The doctor hasn't visited for three days. I begin to think the girl is malingering. I hear her and Beau laughing and having a great time in her room as I walk by. I mean to call on her tomorrow."

"Let me know what she looks like," Josh said.

"Beau calls her uncommonly pretty. I expect that is what you want to know."

"But pretty in what style? Is she dark-complexioned like her brother, or a blonde? Beau

153

is tall—I don't like ladders of ladies." He gave Esther's diminutive frame a close scrutiny as he proffered this preference.

"I will be sure to let you know, Josh."

"You do that."

That evening Beau took dinner in the dining room and stopped at Esther's table on his way out. "My sister is feeling better and asked me to invite you upstairs this evening."

"I'll make a short visit. I don't want to tire her."

"She is feeling much better. In fact, she speaks of taking a run into London tomorrow to hire a costume for the ball."

Lady Brown's eyebrows rose in shock. "Traveling so soon after an illness! Do you think that wise, Mr. Fletcher?"

"It's not much of a journey, and my chaise is well sprung. I shan't let her tire herself."

"Surely there is something in the attics she could wear, Esther."

"You are welcome to have a look, Beau," Esther agreed.

"I'll tell her."

Before long Esther went tapping at Miss Fletcher's door and was shown in by Beau. Her eyes flew to the chaise, where a bright-eyed young lady with blond curls and long-lashed blue eyes sat smiling shyly at her. Her face was angelic, with pretty dimples and white teeth. She had a coverlet drawn over her; beneath it she wore not a nightgown but a fashionable mulled muslin. She was not what Esther expected, somehow. There was none of the dash and charm of her brother. Other than the blue eyes, there wasn't much similarity between them.

Beau introduced them and smiled as Esther welcomed his sister belatedly to the inn and inquired for her health. "I hope you are well enough to attend the ball on Friday," she said.

"I never felt better. I could run a smock race if Beau would let me out of this room. He is taking me to London tomorrow to hire a costume for the masquerade. How are you going to the ball, Miss Lowden?"

They discussed costumes. Esther invited them both to ransack the attics, but it was soon clear that returning to London was what Cathy had in her heart. "It's so exciting." She smiled, eyes sparkling. "I never saw so many stores in my life, and with such lovely things in them." As she talked, she twisted her fingers in her hair, poked at her fingernails, rubbed her nose, and performed a dozen other ill-bred maneuvers. She was one of those vulgar girls who couldn't be still a minute.

She hopped up from the chaise to show Miss Lowden some of her purchases. There were bonnets and shawls, patent slippers and gloves, bottles of perfume, fans, and ladies' toys of all sorts. Shopping was obviously the girl's passion, but soon Esther began to suspect there was another passion awaiting her in London.

"My Cathy tells me she has found herself a beau," her brother said to Esther. "A captain of the Guards, if you please."

"That was quick work!" Esther exclaimed. "You were only there for a few days, were you not?"

Cathy darted a guilty look at her brother, making Esther suspect the young man had been picked up in some unladylike manner. "Captain Williams was a neighbor at home in Northumberland," Beau explained. "It was not quite so unseemly as you are thinking, Esther. But you won't have time to

155

meet your captain when we go to London, Cathy. It will be just a quick trip to pick up your costume."

Cathy wandered to the window, thence to the mirror to pat her curls. "And a new bonnet. You promised me a new bonnet, Beau," she said over her shoulder.

"Indeed I did, and you shall have it. Perhaps you would accompany us, Esther?" he suggested.

A trip to London was always welcome, and with the ball approaching, Esther wanted a few frills for her own toilette. The live flowers for her costume would wilt uncommonly fast, and silk flowers were not available locally. "I shouldn't mind going for a few hours," she said.

They talked awhile and tried to become acquainted. Unfortunately the ladies had little in common. Cathy was not interested in books or local history or such ladylike occupations as painting, embroidery, or playing the piano. Cards were declared a "dead bore." She inquired for the shops and asked whether there would be waltzing at the ball. She did a few waltz steps to show Esther she was familiar with the moves. After a glass of wine and half an hour's desultory talk, Esther escaped. "Let us meet early for breakfast downstairs tomorrow, Miss Fletcher," she suggested.

"Better for Cathy to rest up for the trip, I think," Beau decided. "She'll dine here, and we'll meet at . n." Cathy gave an impatient pout and pulled at her curls.

Esther thought the girl's restlessness might be due to her long incarceration in the room. Beau was overly cautious of her health. There didn't seem to be a thing wrong with her but boredom. He escorted Esther to the door and thanked her for coming. She stopped off to visit Lady Gloria and her aunt to pass a little time. They were not playing cards that evening, but gossiping.

"It gave me quite a turn, I can tell you!" Lady Gloria was saying.

Esther clenched her jaw for the latest injury inflicted on her client. What was it this time? A fly in her soup, curdled cream, damp sheets?

The birdlike head turned to the door. "Ah, here she is now. I was just telling your aunt, Esther, that you have a stowaway in your attic. I was up looking for a costume—Mr. Ramsay gave me permission—and what did I see in the corner but a wad of old clothes made into a mattress, and a bottle of wine. In the corner beneath the east turret window. There were bread crumbs scattered about, too. That will encourage rats, my dear. I told Mr. Ramsay to clean it up."

Esther stared in consternation. "In my attic? Who on earth could it have been?" she asked.

"Your manager thinks it was Captain Johnnie. Lud, to think of him being right above our heads, and none of us knowing a thing about it."

"When did this happen?"

"Just before dark, dear. There was still twilight at the windows. Of course I wasn't alone. One of the upstairs girls came with me. We had Mr. Ramsay up to look around. He'll tell you all about it."

"Why was I not called?"

"You were with Miss Fletcher. What is she like?"

"A pretty ninny," Esther said, already opening the door. "Oh, incidentally, Auntie, I shall be going to London with them tomorrow. I want to pick up a few things for the ball."

Making a grand appearance at the ball was of

prime importance, and Lady Brown decided to permit the trip. "Oh, dear! Make sure you are back well before dark."

Esther fled down to Buck's office. "Buck, what is this about Captain Johnnie hiding in our attics?"

Buck shook his head and expelled air through his pursed lips. "Someone was there, no denying. He had himself a bed made up and two empty wine bottles on the floor. He must have made quite a stay of it."

"Has anyone seen a stranger about the place?"

"We're pretty busy today, but I haven't seen anyone who wasn't a bona fide guest. It wouldn't be a registered guest. If the man had a room, why would he lie on rags in the attic?"

"I don't know—perhaps . . ."

"What?"

"The attic windows give a pretty good view. You can see the beginning of the heath. If someone was just entering—well, he could saddle up and overtake him, I suppose."

"He wouldn't leave evidence behind that he'd been there."

"He might if he was in a hurry," she suggested. "He could return later and hide the evidence."

"It wouldn't take a minute to shove the rags aside and toss the bottles behind a trunk. It wasn't a regular guest. Someone just taking dinner, perhaps," he said pensively.

"Bother, there were half a dozen strange men at dinner. I think I should speak to Officer Clifford."

"He's gone back to London. Not for good, but he had some office work to do. He said he'd be returning tomorrow morning. But in any case I don't think the man was there today. The bread crusts were dry. A pity none of us has been upstairs recently."

"Your room is right next to the attic staircase. You didn't hear anything?"

"No, but then I'm practically never in my room. Esther, don't you think you and your aunt should return to the dower house? I don't like to think of anything happening to you."

There was a tinge of more than concern in his voice. Esther looked at him uncertainly. She remembered Joshua's suggestion that Buck was dangling after her. "We'll be fine," she said, and walked away to the other side of the room.

Buck followed after her. His hand seized her elbow and turned her around. "No point taking chances. You have me here to take care of our inn."

Our inn. The words struck her oddly. When had *her* inn become *our* inn? His hand slid down her arm, grabbing her fingers for a brief squeeze. "Do it, for me," he urged.

She pulled her hand away. "Don't be ridiculous. Now, more than ever, I must be here. I don't want any calamity to befall when Fletcher is on the verge of an offer."

"Eh?" he asked sharply. "Has he offered for you?"

"No, for the inn! He has not offered, but he is serious about buying it."

"Oh," he said sheepishly. "That gave me quite a turn. I will be out of a job when he takes over. At least he didn't mention keeping me on. I didn't ask outright. Not sure I'd like to work for him. I mean, it wouldn't be the same as working for you. I fancy I'd just take off, perhaps go up to London to make my way there."

Esther mistrusted that calflike shine in his eyes. "Let's go up to the attic and have a look around," she said in a businesslike voice.

"I already checked it pretty thoroughly. Nothing there but the wine bottles and the pile of rags. Nothing to tell who was using them."

For the first time since she opened the inn, Esther felt uncomfortable with Buck. She sensed something new in his manner and wondered if he was casting eyes in her direction. It was too ridiculous to consider. She was letting Josh put ideas in her head. She discussed only business during the rest of the meeting, asking him about the names circled in the newspaper.

"I was just doodling. I hoped those noble travelers might put up with us. I was figuring what rooms would suit them. I often do it, not that we get all the names I mark."

Esther soon left. Going to the attic after dark held no allure whatsoever. She didn't go till the next morning, bright and early. She paced immediately through the first rooms to the east turret. She had to move a trunk and stand on it to check the view from the window. She could see for over a mile. The main road led past the inn toward the heath. It was an excellent spot for spying out carriages entering that perilous area. Her guest had been Captain Johnnie, not a doubt of it.

She clambered down and began to shove the trunk back against the wall. Wedged against the wainscoting was a cigar stub. She picked it up and rubbed it between her fingers. It was still moist enough that it didn't crackle. It was fairly fresh, then. She sniffed the air. No scent lingered, but she had no very clear idea how long ago Captain Johnnie had smoked it. Her mind ran over possible known suspects. Joshua didn't smoke cigars, nor had she ever seen Meecham with one. Fletcher didn't smoke them. No one she knew did, not even Buck. Not that he—

The hair on her scalp began to lift, causing a strange, prickling sensation. No, it couldn't be Buck. He was afraid of his own shadow. She could hardly induce him to ride to the heath with her when she had planned her unsuccessful Wrotham trick. Besides, he didn't smoke cigars. He was always in the office. Of course his apartments were right next to the attic stairs. . . .

She ran downstairs as if the Royal Scamp himself were after her and bolted her bedroom door. Her heart was pounding. She paced the room, running in her mind over anything that might support Buck as a new suspect. Captain Johnnie usually struck in the middle of the night. Buck could have slipped out of the inn. He was a local man and knew all the nearby places where a mount might be hidden. His own mount was a chestnut, which would look black at night. His father's farm was only a mile away—a safe place to hide his loot, in one of the farm buildings. He needed the money more than anyone else she could think of.

As she thought, smaller details returned to plague her. Lady Gloria said she had stopped by Buck's office the night the Higginses were attacked, but that he wasn't in. Buck said he had bolted the door to avoid her visit—but had he? Had he been out attacking the Higginses? She thought of the gold wagon theft, the largest and most heinous of Johnnie's crimes. That one had occurred at dawn, and no one had any alibi except that he had been in bed asleep. How could Buck expect to spend so much unexplained money? *I'd just take off, perhaps go up to London to make my way there.*

The worst of suspecting Buck was that she couldn't even discuss it with anyone till Officer Clifford returned. The rest of her acquaintances, Joshua for instance, would either laugh her to scorn, or if they believed her—she thought of Beau—they'd leave her inn. Beau wouldn't expose Cathy to such danger. Perhaps she could tell Joshua. She continued pacing and thinking. The survivor from the gold robbery said there had been two men. Who would Buck's partner be? One large man and one smaller, they said. Buck was tall but slight of frame. He hadn't any close men friends. Only his cousin, Joshua. A large man. The more she thought, the blacker everything looked, till in the end she half believed Joshua and Buck between them were terrorizing the whole neighborhood.

It was ridiculous. They were both honorable gentlemen. Honorable and greedy, in Joshua's case. Honorable and very poor in Buck's. It must gall him, to be sunk to working at the inn. He had been born to better things. If he hadn't fought with his father . . . But he had and was cut off without a sou.

She remembered the newspaper she had taken from Buck's office a week before. He had circled two items in it—announcements of the two noble carriages that would be passing. So that was why he had done it! And slipped up into the attic to watch from the turret window when the carriages passed. She must tell Officer Clifford about that tomorrow before she left for London. A day away from the troubles of the inn was beginning to look more desirable by the minute. She wouldn't give up that small sliver of pleasure. Let Bow Street handle Captain Johnnie. She didn't want to have anything else to do with him.

Chapter Twelve

Officer Clifford was sitting in a far corner of the dining room alone when Esther went downstairs the next morning. "Did you have a pleasant visit in London, Mr. Clifford?" she asked.

"I had a fruitful visit. I did."

She looked expectant, but his impassive face told her nothing, and she hastened on with her own business. "I'm off to London myself today with the Fletchers. I must have a word with you before I leave. Wait for me in the office." She hurried breakfast and went to the office while Buck was still eating, to ensure privacy with Clifford. He was waiting, as requested, when she popped in. She opened her budget, telling him of the visitor in the attic.

"That don't look like the work of a guest now, does it?" he asked. She continued her tale, showing him Buck's newspaper with the two names circled, and mentioning that Buck had the rooms next to the attic door. With her face flushed pink from embarrassment, she even revealed having seen Joshua Ramsay and Mr. Meecham on the heath and punctiliously repeated their excuse for being there.

"Mr. Ramsay mentioned it to me," Clifford told

her. "After you was so foolish as to announce in public that the Wrothams would be coming after dark," he added snidely.

That was clever of Joshua, she thought, but who was to say he hadn't still planned to relieve the Wrothams or any other stray travelers of their money? "I think we ought to include all possible suspects," she said. "Everyone. Even Joshua Ramsay should not be above suspicion."

Mr. Clifford looked at her as though she were a Bedlamite. "And the Prince of Wales, too, I daresay." Esther ignored this piece of impertinence and hastened her departure. "So you're off to London today with the Fletchers, eh? A bit of shopping for the ball, I expect?"

"Precisely."

"The little lady is recovered, is she?"

"Much better, thank you."

"I haven't seen her about."

"You will. We are leaving at ten."

"Quite pretty, I hear."

"Yes, a lovely young blonde."

He nodded his head sagely and smiled. "Ah."

At five to ten Fletcher descended to the dining room and Esther hailed him. "I am all ready and waiting, Beau." She smiled. Despite some misgivings about leaving the inn for a day, she was more than ready for a break. Captain Johnnie had robbed her of enough pleasure this spring. She would not let him spoil her little jaunt to London as well.

"Excellent. Shall we go?"

"But where is your sister?"

"She's waiting in the carriage."

"Oh, I didn't see her come down."

"Your aunt told me you were in Buck's office. I

didn't want Cathy loitering around the lobby, causing a distraction."

Esther hardly felt the girl was pretty enough to cause a riot, but she knew Beau was uncommonly protective of his sister, and she left after saying good-bye to her aunt.

In the carriage Cathy was as bright-eyed and restless as a squirrel. "You must tell me all about the masquerade, Miss Lowden," she said.

Esther passed the first mile with a recital of the decorations and her own costume.

"Who will be attending? Will there be many eligible gentlemen?"

Beau smiled. "I have already informed Cathy of the local bachelors. It is guests from afar she is interested in."

Esther mentally sorted through the guest list for bachelors, and to add prestige to the occasion, she related any titles that occurred to her. "It will be a grand do, Miss Fletcher. The Countess of Altrane will probably wear her emeralds—they are worth a fortune. And of course Lady Sumner will be dripping in diamonds. Joshua tells me she glows like a rainbow when she is fully caparisoned."

"Isn't it rather dangerous, having people cross the heath at this time, carrying their jewelry for a fine ball?" Beau asked.

"Joshua has taken every precaution," she said, and outlined the idea of traveling in a caravan and in daylight.

"That sounds an excellent plan," Fletcher said, nodding his head in approval.

As they drew near to London, they all agreed it would be only a short visit. Beau would escort the ladies on their shopping spree in the morning. They would lunch at a hotel, and afterward Beau would leave them to rest in a private parlor for an hour while he attended to matters with his partner in the import business. Esther enjoyed the shopping. She found her silk flowers, along with a few other elegant trifles. Then they were off to the costume store, where Cathy dallied for a full hour between a shepherdess's outfit, whose wide-brimmed straw bonnet was very becoming, and a more dashing but less suitable French historical gown.

"The straw bonnet is very fetching," Esther urged.

"But I don't care for the slippers," Cathy said, pouting. "They look like a child's shoes. And besides, they pinch my toes."

"Wear your own blue patent slippers," Beau suggested. "The gown is blue."

"I do like the bonnet." Cathy smiled.

The shepherdess's outfit was eventually hired, and they continued on to the hotel for luncheon. "Do we have to sit in here?" Cathy asked, pouting, when they went to the private parlor. "We shan't be able to see a thing."

Beau glared, and Cathy went sulking to the table. "I want to keep the straw bonnet, Beau," she said. "Buy it for me from the rental man. You promised me a new bonnet."

"He wouldn't sell it. It goes with the outfit."

"But I want it," she insisted mulishly. "Buy the whole outfit, then."

"What, an outfit you'd never wear again? Don't be foolish."

"I want a straw bonnet, Beau," she said, in the voice of a shrew.

Beau smiled appeasingly. "Oh, very well, we shall buy you a new straw bonnet. I daresay, that will do as well."

Esther thought what the girl wanted was a good box on the ear. Luncheon was a tedious meal, with Cathy leaving her meat and potatoes on her plate and having two desserts to make up. When Beau left them alone to attend to his business, the afternoon became even more annoying. Bored with her captivity, Cathy insisted on leaving their door ajar, and stood beside it, peering into the hallway for "interesting guests," as she explained to Esther. It was only male guests who elicited any interest.

"We should have gone to stay with your cousin," Esther said. She rather wondered why Beau hadn't suggested it.

"That old malkin!" Cathy scoffed. "She keeps me cooped up like a chicken." Then she turned her gaze back to the hall and soon spotted someone she recognized. Esther refused to be lured to the doorway. She had no wish to be presented to the person. He looked a regular seven-day beau, all tricked out in the latest style with a nipped-waist jacket, an excess of gold trinkets jangling from his waistcoat, and an accent that had a noticeable lack of aitches. Where had Cathy met such a creature?

"Where's Beau?" the man asked.

Cathy gave an inaudible answer. The man chatted for a while, taking a few laughing looks at Miss Lowden before leaving. "I'll catch him at the docks, then," he said, and left.

"I thought Beau was going to his office," Esther said when Cathy came back and lounged beside her at the table.

"He had to go to the docks, too, to see about one of his shipments from Canada. He imports lumber and furs, you know."

"Oh, yes, he mentioned it. I hope he won't be too long. If we have still to shop for a bonnet before we leave London, we shall end up crossing the heath after dark. Who was that man at the door, Miss Fletcher?"

"Mitch Tindale. He's a friend of my cousin—the one I was staying with. I met him at the house."

"What does he do for a living?" He did not look like a man of independent means.

Cathy narrowed her eyes and demanded, "What do you mean?"

"Does he work?"

"Oh, no. He's very well off. A regular swell. Shall we call the servant and ask for some wine, Miss Lowden?"

"You've had enough wine. Call for some tea if you just want to pass the time."

Cathy scowled but jerked the cord, and when the servant appeared, she ordered tea and macaroons, while Esther flipped through a new copy of *La Belle Assemblée* she had picked up while shopping. It was four o'clock before Beau came back, full of apologies for the delay.

"Now can I get my new bonnet?" Cathy asked.

"It's rather late," Esther pointed out. "Why don't you try the shops at home, Miss Fletcher?"

"In that little puddle of a place? They wouldn't have anything I'd be caught dead in."

Esther adjusted her provincially purchased bonnet and said through thin lips to Beau, "Let's get on with it, then, or we'll be here all day."

"We'll leave our parcels here at the inn," Beau said, "and have them put in our carriage."

After visits to three milliner's shops, Cathy finally found a straw bonnet to suit her. The selection had taken a full hour, and the bonnet was ghastly, loaded down with daffodils, poppies, and cornflowers. "What do you think, Miss Lowden?" Cathy asked.

"Lovely," Esther assured her, as approval seemed the fastest way to get home.

When they returned to the hotel, Cathy suddenly found her stomach felt queasy.

"Oh, Lord, it's all those desserts." Beau sighed.

"If I could just lie down for half an hour . . ."

"No!" Esther exclaimed. "Good God, it's after five already. We'll never get home at this rate."

"Perhaps a cup of tea would settle her stomach," Beau suggested.

Yet another pot of tea was ordered. Cathy recovered sufficiently to prance around in her new bonnet, making faces at herself in the mirror. Beau turned apologetically to Esther. "Sorry for the delay, but we don't want her to be sick in the carriage. Cathy tells me a caller stopped around while I was away."

"Yes."

"I don't doubt the little hussy slipped him a message we would be here. She might have sent a note from your inn."

"She did watch the door rather closely, now you mention it. Surely he isn't the fellow from the Guards you mentioned."

Beau laughed. "Lord, no. He's some friend of the aunt Cathy was staying with. I haven't met him. You sound disapproving, Esther. Is he not— gentlemanly?"

"Not very."

"I shall make sure she's kept away from him. You see now why I was so eager to have her with me. I'm afraid Auntie didn't watch her as closely as I would like. The girl's manners have become atrocious. I have suggested she model herself on you."

Esther, unimpressed at this flattery, drew out her watch. "What's keeping that tea?"

"It's getting so late—we really ought to have a bite before we leave, or Cathy will take into her head to make us stop somewhere else. She only pecked at her lunch. Once we leave London, there's nothing but the Black Knight, and I can hardly take you there."

Cathy turned and looked over her shoulder. "Did you suggest we have a bite, Beau? What a good idea. I'm starved."

"If we're all attacked by Captain Johnnie on the way home, pray don't put the blame on me," Esther said, and crossed her arms to show she was peeved with the pair of them.

Coming with the Fletchers had been a wretched idea. Beau was well enough, but his sister showed clearly that the family was not what she was used to. They would probably do quite well with the inn, however, and if Beau made her a good offer, she would accept.

Twilight was falling when they pulled out of London. Before long the carriage was racing through the starry blackness of Hounslow Heath. Overhead a pale moon shone, silvering the shrubs and low-lying mist that clung to the ground. The road wound like a ribbon, white and flat, through the waste track of heath, to disappear into a tunnel of tall trees ahead. The only sounds were the rattle of wheels and the regular clop-clop of the horses' hooves. Tension coiled, snakelike, in Esther's breast. Cathy was nervous, too. She clung to her brother's sleeve in the dark coach.

Esther decided to say what they were all thinking. "If Captain Johnnie strikes, that stand of trees is where he'll attack. It gives excellent cover for a highwayman. We shouldn't have left London so late."

"I promised your aunt I'd have you home tonight," Beau Fletcher reminded her.

"What you actually promised is that we'd be home safe before dark," Esther corrected.

The shadowy form of Beau Fletcher across from her spoke in his usual lively accent. "Why, Esther, I've heard you say a dozen times you'd like to meet Captain Johnnie! What is there to fear? We've taken the precaution of leaving our money behind—you ladies with the milliners and drapers, and I with the bank. You aren't wearing any significant jewelry, and you have me to protect your honor."

"I love my new straw bonnet," Cathy said, perhaps fearing a highwayman would steal it.

Esther found it odd that Beau Fletcher, so dashing and intelligent, should have a perfect widgeon for a sister. If she had to hear once more how much Cathy loved her new straw bonnet, she would crown her. The bonnet was hideous and entirely unsuited to her years. But then, Cathy was young, and a country girl. No doubt the miscellany of flowers and black velvet ribbons struck her as the height of elegance.

Suddenly Beau leaned forward, his head at an alert angle. "Did you hear something?" At that moment the moonlight was cut off as they entered the tunnel of trees. Branches met in an arch overhead, casting them into pitch blackness. Esther knew that this tree tunnel extended for some three or four hundred feet.

They all listened tensely. The whispering of the

boughs mingled with the sounds of the carriage. Nothing else. No hoof beats of a highwayman's mount, no jingling of harness, no warning shot. "You're frightening us to death, Beau," Esther scolded.

"No, really! Didn't you hear it?" he asked. He had his ear to the open window now, straining for a sound.

It was enough to set Esther's heart pounding, and Cathy was clinging to Beau's sleeve like a limpet. Esther listened again and heard it. It sounded like an echo at first, the mere echo of hoofbeats. Someone was advancing along the road toward them, and she was struck with the cold certainty that it was the legendary Royal Scamp, Captain Johnnie. It had been madness to set out across infamous Hounslow Heath after dark.

It was true she had often said in jest that she would like to meet him. Who wouldn't like to meet a folk hero imbued with an aura of glamour and a history that appealed to ladies of a romantic disposition? The sound of hoofbeats thundered nearer. There was no longer any doubt that a single rider was fast approaching; it remained only to see whether it was Captain Johnnie or someone else. When the shot rang out, they all jumped half a foot from the banquettes. Cathy squealed, and simultaneously the carriage slowed with a lurch.

Captain Johnnie had performed according to his accustomed role, then. He had shot off the driver's hat. If he had killed him, the horses would have bolted instead of slackening pace. Esther was shaking like a *blanc-manger*. Her heart thumped against her rib cage—but at the bottom of all her fright, a spring of excitement coiled. She felt the way she felt when her hunter raced at high wood or wide water. There was danger, but not real fear for one's life. It was an almost unbearable excitement, a tingling up the spine, a shiver along the scalp, and a roiling tumult inside.

"Beau, don't try to be a hero," she cautioned. "Just do whatever he says. They say he doesn't hurt anyone if you do as he says. We don't want to be shot."

The carriage ground to a stop. "Under the carriage, facedown," a peremptory voice commanded. This was another part of Captain Johnnie's routine. He forced the driver under the carriage, to keep him from retaliating. The groom scrambled down from his perch without a word. The women looked to Beau for protection as the sound of Captain Johnnie's boots advanced rapidly to the carriage door. He flung it open, and they gazed at the terror of the heath, the Royal Scamp, Captain Johnnie.

Though he had many imitators, there was no doubt in Esther's mind that this was the genuine article. He looked the way a folk hero should look. The tunnel was all in darkness, but when he ordered them out, the carriage lamps gave enough illumination to show them his outline. He was a tall, straight young man with broad shoulders. Bright eyes glittered behind the mask, and his jaw was square. A fall of white Mechlin lace was at his throat. He removed his hat with a theatrical gesture and bowed low, but with his gun pointed unwaveringly at Beau. His hair was as black as the jet stallion chomping the grass behind him. Captain Johnnie smiled a rakish smile, revealing a flash of white teeth.

"We haven't much money," Beau said, "just this," and he drew his purse from his pocket.

174

The highwayman's authoritative voice commanded, "Open it."

Beau poured a few gold coins into Captain Johnnie's outstretched hand. "Your watch, milord," the captain ordered.

Beau looked mutinous. When he made no move to comply, Esther caught his eye and nodded. He unfastened the watch, but reluctantly, and handed it over.

"Under the carriage, facedown," the highwayman ordered Beau.

"I'll be damned if I will!" Beau declared, and took a pace forward. Captain Johnnie smiled a menacing smile.

For a dreadful moment, it seemed Beau was going to be foolish. Esther's heart was in her mouth. How brave Beau was! She was impressed with his daring, but really, this was no time to flaunt it. The two men stood glaring mutinously at each other. Captain Johnnie's finger moved on his pistol.

"For God's sake, Beau, do what he says," Esther implored.

Captain Johnnie leveled his pistol at Beau's heart. Beau gave a frustrated glance at the ladies and got down to climb under the carriage without further ado.

Then the Royal Scamp turned his gaze to the ladies. His voice was low and silk-smooth. "And now for the ladies." He smiled, speaking softly. His predatory smile caused the hair on Esther's arms to lift in fright.

"I only have three shillings," Cathy said nervously, and shoved them at him.

"Keep them, my sweet." He laughed. "But I'll have your ring, darling."

She pulled her pearl ring from her finger and

placed it in his palm. "Now you, milady," he said, and turned his attention to Esther.

She knew he had seen the locket at her neck. It wasn't worth much money, though it had sentimental value. She unfastened it and placed it in his palm. His fingers brushed hers intimately, then closed over the locket. It had a few garnets, which he perhaps mistook for something more valuable in the dim light. "Money, my dear? Alms for Allah," he suggested, in the crooning voice of a lover.

She opened her purse and gave him her money, approximately five guineas. "You travel light!"

"That's all I have," she assured him. He pocketed the money and jewelry.

"Ah, no, my lovely. You have ruby, wine-sweet lips. I'll have a taste of them, to warm my long, cold night."

He swept her into his arms, the pistol still in his right hand, and his masked face descended. It was warm, despite his talk of cold nights. His lips were more than warm, they burned a ruthless kiss on hers. Just one fierce, hot, sweet kiss. Then he stood back, again removed his hat, and bowed formally. "Many thanks from Captain Johnnie," he said, and laughed. His horse, well trained, sidled closer. Through a mist of terror Esther noticed the horse had a white blaze on its nose. Captain Johnnie put his toe in the stirrup, threw a leg over the horse's back and disappeared into the night. The thunder of hooves thinned to an echo and was swallowed up in the spinney. An owl hooted in the sudden silence.

"He didn't kiss *me*!" Cathy exclaimed, pouting. "What was it like, Miss Lowden?"

Esther threw her head back and laughed. She wanted to believe it was only relief that he was gone, but a surge of exultant joy hinted at remembered pleasure. "It was like wine. No, make that brandy. It was heady. Good gracious!" she exclaimed, as Beau began shuffling out from under the carriage. "Are you all right?"

They helped him and the groom out and brushed them off. Beau was obviously disgusted and perhaps unhappy with his own unheroic behavior. "If I had been alone, I wouldn't tamely have crawled under that rig!" he said through clenched teeth.

"Don't be ridiculous! What other choice did you have?" Esther replied. "I was afraid you were going to refuse, and have us all killed."

"Well, now you've seen him." Beau scowled. "I hope you're satisfied. Brandy, indeed!"

"But I loathe brandy," Esther assured him.

"And you, Cathy! You sounded disappointed that you were spared."

"Oh, no, I'm glad," she said, but a blind man could see she was miffed. There was resentment in the look she gave Esther and in the petulant way she tossed her shoulders.

Esther pulled herself back to propriety and said, "You're fortunate. It was horrid!" She kept her face drawn into a frown till they were back in the carriage, continuing their way eastward to the Lowden Arms.

The attack had to be discussed for the first mile, but as they continued homeward, silence fell. It was late, and they were tired from their day in London. Esther settled quietly into her dark corner and smiled softly to herself. Captain Johnnie's attack had been all a maiden could hope for, but best of all, it meant Joshua could no longer hint Beau was the Royal Scamp. As though anyone in his right mind could possibly believe such a thing. Perhaps there was a little jealousy mixed up in Joshua's charge. Her smile, unseen in the shadows, wore an air of complacency.

When they finally reached the Lowden Arms, it was ten o'clock, and Esther knew her aunt would be on the fidgets, worrying about her. She was half embarrassed about the escapade, and said to Beau, "What do you say we keep quiet about our attack? I don't want everyone quizzing me and asking a million questions."

"Why, Esther! You astonish me!" Beau laughed. "You are the only local lady to have been honored by the rogue, and you want to stifle the story!"

"Just for tonight. I can't face all the questions— Officer Clifford . . ." Her head ached to think of it.

"Why don't you and Cathy slip in the back way? I'll speak to Officer Clifford. He really must be told, you know."

"You're right. You make the report. I'm all for an early night in my bed. I feel as though I'd been beaten by an army."

Esther slipped Cathy in through the kitchen and up the back stairs. Now that it was over and she was free of the chit, Esther's mood lightened, and she found herself giggling like a schoolgirl as they tiptoed down the hall to their rooms.

"I'll see you tomorrow morning," she whispered to Cathy.

"Probably not till the ball. Beau is angry with me. He'll make me stay in my room tomorrow, I know he will. You'll recognize me at the ball, Miss Lowden, in my shepherdess's outfit. Perhaps you will stop by my room, to lighten the boredom of the day."

"Unfortunately I'll be spending most of the day at Heath Abbey helping Joshua."

Cathy gave her an arch look. "Beau won't like that! I shall tease him, to make him jealous. I bet he's been flirting his head off while I wasn't here to watch him." The eyes that regarded Esther wore a crafty, curious light.

"You have a poor opinion of your brother! I assure you there is nothing between us."

Cathy stared in disbelief. "Don't you like him? Everyone likes Beau. He speaks very warmly of you, Miss Lowden."

"We are just friends," Esther said, and left, rather annoyed with the question.

She stopped to let Lady Brown know she was home. Her aunt exclaimed at her lateness and questioned Esther for ten minutes. As Beau was telling the tale of Captain Johnnie's attack, Esther decided to reveal it, and gave a toned-down account of the interlude.

"Just what I would have expected from an outing with the Fletchers," Lady Brown said. "Joshua would never mismanage an affair so badly. They seem very common, Esther."

"Yes, they do. I'm rather sorry I asked them to the ball."

"And if they settle in the neighborhood, we shall have to continue knowing them. But we shall taper off the acquaintance rather quickly."

"Yes, indeed, Auntie," Esther replied ruefully. "After all, we don't want to be on terms of equality with someone who runs an inn."

"No, indeed! Oh, you are joking."

"Just laughing at myself. I'm going straight to bed. Good night, Auntie."

Before she had her parcels unwrapped and put away, there was a tap at Esther's door. She opened it to find not only Officer Clifford but a very overwrought Joshua Ramsay. "Esther, are you all right?" He came storming in, half-scolding and half-worried for her.

"Mr. Fletcher reported the incident, I see. I'm fine, Joshua."

Officer Clifford waited his turn, and when the other two were finished, he spoke to Esther. "It seems you are wrong about Captain Johnnie's being an insider, Miss Lowden. All your other suspects were here at the inn the whole time. Mr. Meecham and—Mr. Ramsay."

Joshua scowled. "*I* am a suspect as well, am I?"

"It was Mr. Buck Ramsay we had discussed previously," Clifford told him, with a wink over Joshua's shoulder to assure her he was the soul of discretion.

"Buck!" Joshua looked shocked, but soon burst into raucous laughter. "What arrant nonsense. You might as well claim the vicar to be his helper. Buck Ramsay—where did this absurd notion come from?"

"It shouldn't be completely ignored," Clifford said. "There are a few points that suggest Ramsay." He enumerated them to Joshua, who still scoffed the idea to scorn.

Clifford shook his head doubtfully. "We can eliminate Mr. Fletcher. I know he was your prime suspect, Mr. Ramsay."

Joshua cocked his head at a quizzing angle. "Can we? He might have arranged this attack to divert suspicion from himself."

"No," Esther said firmly. "He might have subjected *me* to such an ordeal, but not his precious sister. He dotes on her and keeps her wrapped in cotton wool. I am convinced he'd never play such a stunt on her."

180

Clifford worried his lips. "The mysterious sister— I still haven't got a peek at her."

"She'll be at my ball tomorrow night."

"Aye, in a mask."

"And a straw bonnet," Esther said, and fell into a fit of giggles as she considered her day.

Clifford left, and Joshua remained behind a moment, with the door carefully open. "What's the joke?" he asked.

"No joke. It wasn't funny at all. I had a perfectly wretched day, Joshua."

He looked insensibly pleased to hear it but spoke of other things. "What foolishness have you been telling Clifford about Buck?"

"It's not nonsense. He's in a perfect position to enact the role of Johnnie."

"So am I, for that matter."

She looked at him askance. "I know it." Their eyes met. She saw an angry flash in Joshua's and looked away. It seemed suddenly ludicrous that she should suspect him.

Joshua scowled. "I'll be glad tomorrow night when this is all over."

"What do you mean? Nothing will happen tomorrow night. You've taken every precaution, haven't you?"

"I don't think I've overlooked any detail. I'll expect to see you at the Abbey in the morning, Esther. If you feel safe to visit me, that is?" The resentment was still there, burning in him. "Perhaps you'd like to bring Fletcher along to protect you?"

"No, he wouldn't come without Cathy. I'll take my chances that you're the Scamp," she said, and smiled.

"A rag-mannered chit, is she?"

Esther hunched her shoulders. "She's young. Perhaps her officer of the Guards will rub off the rough edges. I hear she has attached one."

"She's a fast worker—faster than some."

Esther read a hint that she was less speedy in bringing him up to scratch, and was swift to retaliate. "Perhaps she's more eager to marry than I am."

Joshua gave her a frowning look and left.

Chapter Thirteen

Esther enjoyed her day at the Abbey, welcoming Joshua's guests and arranging final details for the ball. Many of his relatives were known to her, but his friends were not. She was gratified to learn they were all elegant, fashionable people of good sense and refinement. How fortunate Josh was, having a toe in London society to relieve the tedium of the country. His wife would share that life. Her interest soared to new heights when the Chalmers party arrived. She examined Lady Margaret, who examined her with a similarly alert eye.

Not so young! was Esther's first mental remark. Not so pretty, was the second. But not an antidote by any means. She was tall and elegantly slender, with brown hair and friendly brown eyes, and, of course, an invisible dowry of twenty-five thousand pounds, which was not to be ignored. Esther offered to escort Lady Margaret to her chamber, to allow a longer study of the competition.

"The Abbey is lovely," Lady Margaret said, looking over the banister down to the hall as they mounted the staircase.

"And the park, too—charming. I understand you

are a close neighbor, Miss Lowden? Joshua has often spoken of you."

Obviously he had not "often" spoken without having been frequently in Lady Margaret's company. Esther felt a burning sensation in her chest. She smiled archly and said, "Then you have the advantage of me, ma'am. He has not told me much about you."

"Oh, there is little to tell." She smiled. "There is no adventure in *my* life. We have been friends forever. Till now we have only met in London. My family lives quite far up north."

Esther correctly interpreted the adventure of her own life to refer to the Lowden Arms. She was annoyed that Lady Margaret knew about it, and peered for signs of disapproval. Joshua's inviting the Chalmers to the Abbey for the first time assumed new importance. Was it a precursor to an offer? Before Esther could pose any leading questions, Lady Margaret began to speak of the Royal Scamp. "Do you think he'll show up at the ball?" she asked, eyes sparkling in anticipation. One could certainly not accuse Lady Margaret of a lack of spirit.

"I shouldn't think so. The heath is his bailiwick."

They entered the bedchamber. "What a lovely room! And what a view!" Lady Margaret hastened to the window to gaze out on the park, where another black carriage was just rolling along through the trees. "Isn't it exciting, coming to a country ball? One senses something in the air—a tingle that is lacking in London, where balls are a mere commonplace, all the same, meeting the same people forever."

"Yes, charming," Esther agreed, but she knew

what caused that tingle. It was the knowledge that nearby lurked the infamous Captain Johnnie. She was tempted to tell Lady Margaret of her adventure, but decided against it, as Joshua had kept mum. The ladies chatted a few moments. Each was a little forlorn to discover the other was unexceptionable. A trifle provincial in her manners was the worst Lady Margaret could think. A little older than I would have thought and less pretty was Esther's verdict.

As the day was fine; Joshua had a picnic lunch served outdoors, after which the guests roamed around the Abbey, admiring the monks' walk, the gardens, and the chapel. Esther and her aunt returned to the inn to prepare for the ball and the formal dinner that would precede it. To add to the evening's entertainment, normal evening wear was the dress for dinner, with a change to costume before the ball.

Lady Margaret was slightly relieved to see it was Lady Brown and not Miss Lowden who took the hostess's chair at the foot of the table. Nothing was absolutely settled with Miss Lowden, then. But as the meal continued, she noticed Joshua's eyes roved more frequently down the board to Miss Lowden than to herself. Miss Lowden looked quite pretty in a mint-green gown. She noticed the lack of diamonds at her throat. The girl wouldn't win a second look in London. Her manners were pretty, though. She conversed in a lively but not pert way with both her companions.

Soon Lady Margaret's attention was diverted to her own companion, a Mr. Meecham, who was really quite handsome, and a veteran of the Peninsular War. He seemed rather taken with her. She did some gentle quizzing to discover that he was one of the Meechams from Devonshire—a younger son, but with good prospects at Whitehall. Before the dessert was served, she had mentioned that her father had friends in his department, and Mr. Meecham had requested the first dance of her.

Esther paid less attention to Lady Margaret. Her eyes were busy making an inventory of the jewels at the table. If Captain Johnnie should take into his head to rob Josh's safe that night, he would collect something in the neighborhood of a million pounds. She must warn Joshua to increase the guard on the safe. Near the head of the table Lady Sumner's diamonds resembled a chandelier fallen from the ceiling to take up occupancy of a seat at the table. The Countess of Altrane's emeralds were less luminous. They twinkled from the wattles of the lady's throat, but did not glow. The aging wearers of all this splendor were hardly noticed. They were a pair of fading old dames, mere vehicles for displaying the fabulous jewelry.

After dinner the gentlemen remained behind for port, but the ladies made only a brief visit to the saloon. For this grand occasion they wanted a long toilette. With so many guests in the house, Esther was sharing a room with her aunt. Joshua sent a servant up to assist their dressing. Lady Brown's only change was to put a blue domino and mask on over her evening gown. Esther changed into her Queen of the May outfit, and the servant brushed out her hair and arranged the new silk flowers in it. Excitement flushed her cheeks to rose and lent a glitter to her eyes.

When she was finished, Esther said to the servant, "I'd like to speak to Mr. Ramsay when he leaves the dining room. Ask him to come up, will you please?"

A little later Joshua tapped at her door. She slipped into the hallway. Joshua smiled in approval of her outfit. "You are the Queen of the May," he said. "Enchanting, Esther. White becomes you."

"Oh, thank you," she replied, flustered at the compliment and the way his eyes lingered on her hair, then roved over her face. She spoke on hastily to cover her embarrassment. "But where is your costume?"

"I'll throw a domino over my jacket."

"Original. I had the most *appalling* thought at dinner, Josh. What if Johnnie tries to break into your safe tonight?"

"I only put about the story the jewelry would be kept there. Actually the safe is empty."

"But then, where will you keep the jewelry?"

He gave a teasing smile. "Are you sure I can trust you?"

She pouted. "Don't tell me if you don't want to, but I hope some precautions have been taken."

"He'd never dare attack a private house. That isn't his lay. Everyone is responsible for the safety of his own valuables. I did whisper a word of caution to Lady Altrane and Lady Sumner. They've each brought a spare footman to help guard the valuables. I wish they hadn't worn such costly ornaments, but they tell me they're fully insured. Their rooms are side by side, just down there," he said, tossing his head to the end of the corridor. "In that way they'll be doubly protected. Any commotion in one room will be heard in the other."

"Still, you wouldn't want anything to happen to them while they are under your protection."

"You worry yourself for nothing, Esther. This is your ball. Try, if you can, to enjoy yourself."

"My ball? Don't try to con me into believing

that." She turned back to her door, then tossed over her shoulder before entering, "By the way, I like your Lady Margaret. Very nice."

"Paul thinks so, too. And incidentally, Lady Margaret paid you exactly the same compliment. 'Very nice'. I'm happy you two get along."

"Why?" The word came popping out before Esther got a guard on her tongue. Was he suggesting Lady Margaret would soon inhabit the Abbey?

Joshua gave a maddeningly bland look. "She might become your neighbor one of these days."

"You'd best look lively. Your friend Meecham was rolling his eyes at her over dinner."

"You noticed that, too, did you?" he said, and left, laughing.

Esther felt a churning inside. Between worries that Lady Margaret had attached Joshua, that Captain Johnnie would rob the guests, and that the strawberry ices wouldn't set in time for the midnight dinner, for they were proving obstinate in that respect, Esther was in danger of flying into a temper.

"Shall we go down now?" Lady Brown asked, as soon as she entered the room. "If I am to play hostess, I'd best be at the door early."

Joshua was already at the doorway when they descended. His tall form and broad shoulders were an impressive sight. At some time during his busy day he had been to the barber. His black hair shone in the lamplight. With a smile to remove the harshness from his features, he looked more handsome than usual. He seemed more like the old Joshua, the Joshua who had favored Esther before she opened her inn. This was the London Joshua, wearing his party manners. This was a man she could love and happily marry—if he asked her. He turned and spotted her, nodded, and smiled, and she felt proud at the special mark of recognition. There was something in that smile, a little special warmth.

Esther's services were not required at the door, but she went to entertain the guests, who were gathering to await the opening of the ball. In the Gold Saloon, Henry VIII rubbed shoulders with a pirate in eye patch and kerchief. There were ladies in panniered gowns and elaborate wigs, in the guise of milkmaids and Pierrettes, and one daring lady in a torn gown with a red ribbon around her neck, to show she was a victim of Robespierre's guillotine. But more than anything else there were gentlemen in black dominos and masks, many of them with a wide-brimmed hat to show that they were the Royal Scamp.

The provincial guests arrived promptly, swelling the number of Royal Scamps and milkmaids. Esther recognized Cathy's straw bonnet, the one that came with her outfit. Beau, more original than most of the men, wore his naval officer's uniform and looked extremely gallant. A patch over one eye indicated that for the night he was promoted to admiral and was the celebrated Admiral Nelson, but with both arms intact.

Esther had the pleasure of opening the ball with Joshua. All eyes were on them for the first moments. "What will your Lady Margaret think of this?" she asked.

"You were right to tease me," he said. "Paul beat me to the gun. He secured Lady Margaret for the opening minuet."

"You did ask her, then?" she inquired, in her most offhand manner.

"No, Paul told me."

Esther looked around the room and discovered

Lady Margaret in a Grecian toga that did nothing for her long, slender figure. Paul wore a domino and mask, presumably the one she had discovered in his room when she searched it the week before.

"Does Paul know where the jewels are being kept?" she asked on an impulse.

"I don't recall discussing it with him. Why do you ask?"

"Just curious." The idea that Joshua was the Royal Scamp had dissipated, but Paul was by no means considered innocent.

"I didn't tell my cousin Buck, either, in case it is the Scamp you're worried about. Really, Esther— Buck! How could you be such a gudgeon?"

"Is he here yet? I haven't seen him."

"He just came in. He's borrowed a cassock from my attic and come as a monk. Who's minding the inn tonight?"

"Scott, the head footman, takes over when Buck's away. Oh, there's Officer Clifford. How droll he looks in that wide-striped waistcoat and funny white tie spotted with black. He looks like a clown."

"And with rosettes at the knees of his plush breeches. Thank you for the words of praise, Esther. That's my get-up for the F.H.C. he's wearing. I loaned it to him."

A ripple of laughter escaped. "You mean you actually appear in public in that get-up?"

He peered down at her, smiling at her amusement. "Top of the trees."

"Do all the bucks wear that?"

"No, only those of us who have the privilege of being permitted to the club's exclusive membership."

"I see he can't get anyone to dance with him."

"Clifford isn't here to dance. He's keeping a sharp lookout for trouble."

Esther felt a shiver tremble up her spine. "Do you think there might be trouble?"

"I trust there will, or I've gone to a deal of bother for nothing."

"Any dubious pleasure *I* may take from *my* ball counts for nought, does it?"

Joshua shrugged but looked conscious of his slip. "It's known as killing two birds with one stone."

"Also as putting your foot in your mouth. Never mind, I've known all along this ball wasn't for my benefit. I merely had the honor of working my fingers to the bone for you."

"You'd be happy to have Captain Johnnie behind bars though, wouldn't you?"

"Very happy, but I don't see how you hope to accomplish it, when you've gone to such pains to make a holdup impossible."

"Not impossible, just interesting. Johnnie's no tyro. He'd suspect a trap if we made it easy."

The dance was over, and Joshua strode away. Esther felt as if she were sitting on a patch of nettles. What did he mean by "trap"? There was something going on here that she was unaware of. While the party progressed, she tried to keep her eye on the key players. She could see Buck's round monkish hat through the crowd, the only thing to distinguish him at a quick glance from the dozens of black dominoes. Beau was a little easier to keep an eye on in his naval uniform. Clifford's garish outfit wasn't difficult to spot, lurking round the edge of the room. Paul Meecham was invisible among the other dominoes.

Beau claimed Esther for the first set of waltzes, while his sister, she noticed, danced with Buck.

"This is the first time we've danced together, Esther," he said. "I knew you would be light-footed."

"Cathy waltzes well for a deb. Where did she learn?"

"I expect the waltz has reached Northumberland. It was kind of Buck to stand up with her, as she has so few acquaintances here. I'm indebted to your manager on more than one score. He was kind enough to give us a lift here. I cracked a shaft on my carriage last night during that mad dash home from the heath."

"I'm sorry. I hadn't heard it, as I've been away from the inn so much today. Did anything else of interest happen?"

"Not much. We all took considerable amusement from watching the carriages rumble along to the Abbey here for the party. What a magnificent affair it is. I'm blinded by diamonds." His eyes turned to the blaze of glory that was Lady Sumner leaving for the card room. "What a pity the jewels are all worn by ancients. They should adorn some beautiful young lady, like you."

Beau was a good dancer. Esther enjoyed the waltzes and the compliments. When they were over, he led her to his sister; they changed partners, and Beau took Cathy for a stroll about the room.

Esther and Buck waited for the music to resume. Buck seemed nervous, looking around the sides of the room for something. "My Papa's landed in," he explained. "He'll have something to say about my standing up with Miss Fletcher. At least he'll be happy I've nabbed you for the next dance."

"This might be your chance to make it up with him," she suggested.

"I'm willing, but I won't grovel to him. He must take me as I am."

"Did anything exciting happen at the inn today while I was away?" she asked.

He reported on any clients of interest who had taken rooms, then mentioned Beau's damaged carriage. "It's been a hard day on carriages and nags. I noticed Meecham's mount was missing when I went to get my own rig to come here. His groom tells me the nag threw a splint yesterday, and was left in Josh's stable."

Esther immediately felt a prickle of suspicion. "Was it here when you arrived?"

"I didn't go to the stable. We got out at the front door. Why do you ask?" Her speaking glance told him why. "Don't go looking for trouble, Esther. It will find you soon enough."

"But if it isn't in Josh's stable, Buck—where is it? Is it hidden nearby for Meecham's getaway after he robs the guests?"

"Rubbish!"

"Still, I would very much like to know," she insisted.

Buck ignored her hint. He asked her for the next set, but Esther made an excuse and left. Perhaps it would be better to look for Meecham's mount herself. Buck was not completely free of suspicion. For that matter he could have taken Meecham's mount himself, planning to make his escape on it, hide the loot, and return. She walked down a hallway, into the library, and out the French door into a hedged garden.

Light streamed from all the Abbey windows. Soon she heard the muted strains of music, adding a touch of magic to the soft night breeze. The possible places of concealment were so numerous that she tried to put herself in the Scamp's boots and see how she would plan a fast getaway. Not by the back

193

of the house, where the stable was alive with grooms tonight. No, he would cut through the park, where riding was easy and concealment plentiful, and close by was the public road.

She lifted her white skirts and walked briskly toward the park. He wouldn't have left his mount close enough that its whinnying would be heard by guests arriving. It would be a few hundred yards into the park. As she advanced through the trees, shadows deepened. Was Meecham working alone, or would he have his groom waiting as well? Her heart hammered in her throat, nearly deafening her. The night breeze felt cold against her fevered cheek. When an owl hooted, she jumped a foot into the air. But before long a different sound invaded her ears. It was the soft, satisfied snorting of a horse champing the grass. She darted behind a tree and peered out from behind it. The horse was there, apparently alone. She edged closer, slipping from tree to tree. From a few yards away, she recognized Meecham's mount with the white blaze on its forehead. Captain Johnnie's mount last night had had such a blaze.

Chapter Fourteen

Esther lifted her skirts and tore back to the Hall, uncertain whom she should tell. When she reached the ballroom, she saw Joshua dancing with Lady Margaret. Officer Clifford lounged toward her. "All's quiet so far," he said, from behind his mask.

She drew him aside and told him about Meecham's mount. "Don't worry your head, Miss Lowden. I'll take care of it."

"But if you leave, there will be no one here to watch him."

"Nay, I'm not alone, miss. I have two of my lads rigged out as footmen, and two in dominoes. You just enjoy your ball and leave the dirty work to us. It's what we're paid for."

Esther found the ball about as enjoyable as having a tooth drawn. She felt every moment that something dreadful was going to happen, and to make it worse, she didn't have one perfectly reliable ally. Her eyes roamed from Admiral Nelson to F.H.C. member, from monk to black domino, while the excitement churned. She danced, too, conversing erratically with her partners. Eventually it was time for the midnight supper, and nothing unusual had occurred.

She decided she had destroyed a perfectly good ball for no reason and determined to enjoy the remainder of it. She took what enjoyment she could from sitting at Joshua's table, along with Lady Margaret, Meecham, Lady Brown, and a few of the more exalted guests. Lady Altrane in her emeralds and Lady Sumner in her diamonds were part of the table, along with Lady Gloria in her pearls. With the single exception of the strawberry ices, which Lady Gloria found just a teensy bit liquid, the dinner was excellent. Lobster and champagne added a festive note to the viands.

Yet, Esther felt an undercurrent of something more exciting than just a ball. It was like a magnetic force, and it emanated from Joshua and Meecham. More than once she noticed them exchanging mute but meaningful looks. Their eyes scanned the other tables. Esther tried to follow their line of sight. Was it Buck they were looking at? He sat with his parents, in apparent amity. Officer Clifford? The Fletchers? Some of Clifford's minions? Impossible to say, but they were wary, like jungle cats watching their prey.

Dinner was a prolonged affair, with many courses and several toasts afterward, but finally it was over. The guests complimented Joshua profusely on a perfect ball. Some of the older ones decided they were for bed. "Not so young as I used to be" was heard, along with "I must be up early in the morning. Paper work to look after for parliament." The diamonds and emeralds left the table with the older crowd.

It was effectively over then, Esther assumed, and breathed a sigh of relief. All her anxieties had been for nothing. She had stupidly let her imagination ruin her evening thus far, but she would enjoy the last two hours of dancing. As the musicians tuned their instruments for a country dance, Esther scanned the floor for a partner. She had only had one dance with Joshua. Another one would not be out of place. There were literally dozens of black dominoes, but as her eyes darted from one to the other, she could not find Joshua. He should be easy to spot, as he was taller than most and his hair was so dark.

Perhaps he was speaking to the housekeeper about the retiring guests. She hadn't danced with Meecham. She had noticed he was a good dancer. After a quick run around the room, she realized Meecham was missing as well, and a tingle of apprehension disturbed her newfound peace. Soon she discerned there was no Admiral Nelson, either. This was too many missing bodies for mere coincidence. Perhaps Buck knew what was going on. She discovered his round monk's hat and made her way toward him.

"Where is everyone?" she demanded.

"Eh?" He looked around the crowded room. "The old folks have hit the tick. Papa has gone home. He invited me to call next week. He ain't happy with me, but at least he's speaking."

"But where are the others?"

"Looks like the rest of 'em are here, waiting for the music to begin. I meant to stand up with Miss Fletcher again. Have you seen her?"

"Not since dinner."

"Do you know, Esther, I still don't know what she looks like? I'd like to get her to take off her mask. She's a light stepper. Dashed pretty curls she has."

Esther looked all around for the shepherdess and soon knew she wasn't in the room.

"Went upstairs to tidy her toilette, I daresay,"
Buck decided. "I'll keep an eye peeled on the staircase, or Meecham will beat me to her. I notice he
watches her like a hawk."

"Oh, no, I'm sure he has Lady Margaret in his
eye."

"Rubbish. Miss Fletcher don't take a step that he
ain't after her like a fox after a chicken. I even saw
him follow her out for a breath of air before dinner.
If her brother hadn't been with her, he would have
tried to steal a kiss. A bit of a commoner, that lad.
His room at the inn is like a pigsty. The servants
tell me he's broken the door frame, to say nothing
of that grease on the carpet."

Esther had very little interest in Miss Fletcher.
She withdrew to a quiet corner to watch and think.
Clifford knew Meecham's horse was tethered outside. Perhaps checking up on it accounted for the
Bow Street officer's absence. Her nervousness
mounted. There was something wrong, but try as
she might, she couldn't put a finger on it. Lady Altrane and Lady Sumner had retired, so their jewels
were safe. Or were they? Was the robbery going to
occur in their chambers, after they were asleep?

Esther rose and headed for the great staircase.
The doors at the end of the hallway that Joshua
had pointed out as theirs were closed, silent. Lamps
along the corridor gave a dim light, enough to show
her no one was there. Yet a tingling along her scalp
spelled danger. She couldn't be imagining it. A
breeze stirred at the window at the end of the hall,
lifting the hair on her arms. Curtains billowed over
the heavy chest below the window. The very silence
was unnerving. Wouldn't people preparing for bed
make some small sound at least? She felt as if the
very shadows were watching her.

She would just run down the hall and put her ear to their doors. She'd look a fool if she were caught, but a sixth sense told her things were not what they appeared. From behind Lady Altrane's door she heard a low, spiteful laugh. "And the bracelet, milady. Alms for Allah." Captain Johnnie! Esther froze to the spot, momentarily unable to move. He was there, robbing Lady Altrane, and there wasn't a soul around to help her.

While she stood, summoning courage and trying to think what to do, the door opened and a masked man in a black cape and broad-brimmed hat came out, stuffing a string of emeralds into his inner pocket. He stopped a moment when he saw her. His pistol rose, and she found herself staring into eternity at the round, black hole of the muzzle.

"One word, and it will be your last," the Scamp cautioned. The deadly menace of his voice held her silent.

What was he waiting for? He glanced over his shoulder. Behind him, a smaller masked man appeared, also in a black hat and cape, and with a strand of diamonds hanging from one gloved hand, a pistol in the other.

Esther stood, terrified into immobility. A strange ringing in her ears nearly deafened her, as she studied the two masked men, one noticeably smaller than the other. This was the pair who had robbed the gold wagon and killed two men in the doing of it. They would kill her without a second thought if she tried to stop them. The men didn't say a word. They looked at each other uncertainly, as though silently deciding what to do with her. Their silence was more terrifying than threats.

The taller one looked at the window, then at the smaller man. He tossed his head toward the window, indicating their means of escape. Was it Mee-cham? He had worn a domino. The size was right, and the firm jaw. Yet not so firm as the jaw of the man who had kissed her on the heath. If she could hear him speak at close range . . .

He stared at her, his eyes two glittering slits behind the mask. "You first," he growled to his helper, but in an unrecognizable voice. "You, right behind," he ordered Esther.

She stared. The smaller man put the diamonds in a pocket and shoved her toward the window. "I can't jump! I'll break my legs!" Esther objected, but in a quaking voice.

"With luck, it'll be your neck." The tall one laughed.

The other drew aside the velvet curtains and she saw a stout rope tethered to the legs of the heavy chest. He drew out a drawer of the chest, clambered nimbly up on top and let himself out, while the other kept his pistol trained on Esther. Awkwardly she climbed onto the chest, out the window, and let herself down the knotted rope. Her fingers burned, and the rough hemp caught at her gown, but Esther didn't notice. What are they going to do when they get me outside, away from the safety of the house? she wondered.

The smaller man was waiting, silently pointing his pistol at her, when her feet hit the ground. Within seconds the taller one joined them. Esther looked around for a weapon or the best means of escape. While her eyes scanned the Abbey for a doorway and she gauged her chances of reaching it without being shot, another masked, caped man shot from the shadows, and another. The roadway was suddenly littered with replicas of Captain Johnnie, lending a nightmare quality to the affair.

"Grab him, lads!" Officer Clifford's voice called out.

In the same instant the real Captain Johnnie pulled Esther in front of him for protection.

"Hiding behind a lady's skirts," Clifford scoffed. "Now is that any way for a Royal Scamp to behave?"

The tallest of the masked men lunged forward, a string of oaths spluttering from his lips. Through a miasma of terror Esther recognized Joshua. "You touch her and I'll hound you to hell and back. You won't get away this time!"

Captain Johnnie uttered a menacing laugh and cocked the pistol. "One move, and I plug her," he warned. Joshua came to a halt, as if frozen. Esther heard his heavy breaths and saw the clenching of his jaw. "Throw your pistols at her feet—nice and easy."

Esther felt the sharp pressure of the gun's muzzle against her spine. Clifford and the other men kept their pistols. "Now!" Johnnie barked.

"For God's sake, do it!" she implored, and four guns fell with a thud at her feet.

"The other one's sneaking away!" someone called. It sounded like Meecham.

Esther turned and blinked as she noticed a pair of blue patent slippers flashing beneath the black cape as the smaller man moved rapidly over the ground. Meecham disappeared into the shadows of the park, hounding after the Scamp's assistant.

"Your mount won't be coming to you as you planned," Clifford crowed.

"Then you'll be bringing me one from the stable. Now!" His voice boomed out, full of authority. To reinforce the command, he jabbed the pistol into Esther's back, causing her to jerk forward.

"Do as he says," Joshua Ramsay ordered. He surveyed the scene. Johnnie had Esther, but even without Clifford and Meecham, there were the footman-runner and himself against Johnnie. What they required was a distraction. He surveyed his options; all of them put Esther in too much jeopardy. One nervous spasm of the Scamp's finger, and she was dead.

Esther studied the men in front of her, counting up characters. Meecham chasing through the park, Joshua here, Buck innocently waiting in the ballroom for Cathy. The masked man was Fletcher, then, and the small assistant his sister, in her blue patent slippers. She had let that simpleton of a Cathy hold her at gunpoint, when she should have scratched her eyes out. If she had known, she would have leapt on her before Fletcher got down the rope. But who had attacked her and the Fletchers that night on the heath? Some friend of Beau's, put up to it to fool her?

Captain Johnnie's glamour and mystique fell from him. He was just Beau Fletcher dressed up in costume. She'd be damned if she'd be afraid of him. Yet the pistol snuggled against her spine held her quiet. The edgy silence stretched. Fletcher saw Joshua eying the pistols.

"Pick up the pistols, one by one, and throw them into the park," he said to Esther.

He leaned forward, holding his pistol against her while she lifted one pistol and threw it, but not very far. She reached for another. Did she dare risk turning it against Johnnie? Perhaps if she threw herself to the ground . . . But Johnnie didn't usually kill his victims if they did as he said. Her life was worth more than Lady Sumner's diamond necklace. She threw the second pistol beside the first.

Joshua watched, silently willing Esther not to do anything foolishly reckless. Meecham would have the sister in custody. That was a trump for them. And he had removed their waiting boat from the dock. That would hold up their escape. There was time to catch them yet. If only Esther didn't do something foolish. Perspiration beaded his brow, and he pulled off his mask.

"Now, another pistol," Beau ordered. "I'll take it. Hand it to me. Don't turn around. Just put it behind your back."

This was her chance. Esther carefully took hold of the pistol handle, put it behind her back, aimed the muzzle at Fletcher, released the safety catch, and pulled the trigger. A deafening shot rang out. Beau gave a leap and a howl of pain, followed by a string of obscenities. He dropped his pistol and clutched at his wounded hand. When she turned, Esther saw blood dripping from his fingers. In the same instant Joshua threw himself on the howling Scamp, adding his own profanities to the scene.

Officer Clifford arrived with a mount and grinned at the brouhaha. He dismounted and began gathering up pistols. "Well done, lads!" he congratulated.

Joshua turned Fletcher over to the runner and rushed to Esther. He grabbed her by the arms first, then pulled her tightly against his chest, one hand stroking her back. "Are you all right, darling? Did he hurt you?" He looked down at her, and she saw the love and fear glowing in his eyes.

"No, I'm all right," she assured him.

Josh's fear gave way to relief and was soon finding an outlet in anger. "Why did you go bumbling upstairs? We had everything set! You might have been killed," he scolded. The sting of his words was softened by a reassuring hug.

"You should have told me!" Esther exclaimed.

"I didn't want you involved."

"Not involved? He was staying at *my* inn! *I* was more involved than anyone."

"Yes, you were happy to involve yourself with a blasted criminal. Running off to London with him. Why do you think I had this ball? To get him away from your inn for the capture!"

"I knew you weren't having it for me."

"I had it to get that creature out of your inn. I didn't want to have him arrested there, and shoot up half your customers."

Clifford nudged Joshua with his elbow. "My lad's taking Fletcher into the roundhouse. I'm going after Meecham and the sister. Are you coming with me? Not that I need help to arrest a woman. The sly minx. I know what face I'll see under her mask. The same blond lightskirt who gave Johnnie an alibi at the Black Knight. I knew when Miss Lowden told me she was a blonde who she was. That's why she's been at such pains to avoid showing herself— never leaving her room unless she had Fletcher run downstairs first to see I wasn't around."

"I doubt she is his sister," Joshua said. "His bit of muslin is more like it."

Esther remembered the loving laughter from Cathy's room, and Beau's treatment of her, which was more uxorious than anything else. "The wretch! I wager he has no intention of buying the inn."

"I should hope not!" Joshua exclaimed.

"Are you coming or no?" Clifford demanded.

"I'll take Miss Lowden into the house."

204

"I'm going with Clifford," Esther said.

"That you are not, missie. One debacle a night is enough," Clifford told her. "Take her away," he said to Joshua, in much the same tone he had used to his minion for the removal of Captain Johnnie.

Clifford shook his head as the young couple went toward the Abbey, arguing like a pair of fishwives.

Chapter Fifteen

It was four o'clock in the morning before the ball was over and the guests retired. Other than Lady Altrane and Lady Sumner, no one was aware of what had happened in their rooms and outside the Abbey. Those stalwart dames had volunteered their services, with the proviso that paste replicas of their treasures be used for the deception. They had no fear for their lives, as they were instructed by Officer Clifford to hand the jewels over without an argument. Clifford's hirelings posed as their footmen for the visit. The ladies also submitted to being tied and gagged, on the understanding that Joshua would send a servant to untie them as soon as the Scamp had left the house. The rooms on either side of theirs were occupied by listening helpers. Lady Sumner had some hopes of a kiss from the midnight bandit for a reward, but was disappointed. Captain Johnnie used some discrimination in that matter.

Buck took Lady Brown and Lady Gloria back to the inn with him, and Esther remained behind to await Meecham's return.

"Joshua will drive me home soon, Auntie. Don't wait up for me," Esther said.

This unusual procedure found no objection from the hopeful matchmaker. She wouldn't have objected if Esther had said she meant to move into the Abbey as a laundress. Joshua could do no wrong. "Don't be too late" was her only warning.

It was already four-thirty before Meecham and Clifford came back to relate the final outcome of the affair and straighten out a few details. Joshua called for coffee, in an attempt to keep everyone's eyes open another half hour.

"How long have you known Fletcher was Captain Johnnie?" Esther asked Clifford.

"He was the prime suspect from day one."

"But he had an alibi for the time of the Higginses' attack."

"That one wasn't Captain Johnnie's work," he told her. "There are plenty of scamps on the heath, many of them using Johnnie's tricks. The minute he conned you into showing him all the nooks and crannies of your inn, Fletcher rose to the top of my list. He pulled the same stunt at the Black Knight and hid his loot in the attic. The girl he calls his sister, Cathy Barker, gave him his alibi at the Black Knight, which put me off a little. Actually she was his accomplice in the gold robbery."

"She isn't his sister?" Esther asked.

"She is Fletcher's light-o'-love and, sometimes, his accomplice. London is her usual ground, but she follows Johnnie about here and there. She knew I would recognize her, so kept her phiz hidden when he brought her here. Her papa was the famous highwayman, Black Barker. She comes by her calling honestly."

"She won't hang," Meecham said, "but she'll do a stretch at Bridewell. It was Fletcher who shot the guards on the gold wagon. The night he went to

London, ostensibly to fetch her, they met at the Black Knight and went after the gold. I fancy she is the one who learned it was moving at that time."

"The likes of Johnnie and his woman have helpers in critical places," Clifford said. "They could have been in league with one of the guards he shot. The man would tip him the clue as to when the gold was moving, planning to get his share. That is the likeliest thing—then Johnnie got rid of the weak link and kept all the gold for himself. The girl confessed they hid it not far from where he ditched the carriage in the Thames. She's giving evidence to save her own skin. No honor among thieves, whatever they may say."

"Is Fletcher an ex-navy man?" Esther asked.

"The Admiralty has no record of a Captain Fletcher. There was a seaman of the name, posted to Canada."

"He did seem to know something about Canada," she remembered.

"As Seaman Fletcher is a deserter, I figure he's our man. That would explain why he planned his getaway by boat tonight. He had a tidy skiff anchored at the bottom of the Abbey cliff, manned by his groom. I had him followed when he took you to London, Miss Lowden. He made a visit to the docks."

"He said he had some importing business to look into."

"That is when he arranged for the boat, so we knew how he planned his getaway," Clifford continued. "Young Meecham tethered his mount in the park to go after them if they evaded us here at the house. We were set to pounce on them as they crawled out the window, but of course when we saw they had you with them, we had to improvise." A glint of annoyance from his brown eyes was the only chastisement Esther received.

She returned the glint with interest. "I wouldn't have been with them if you had told me what was going on!"

"We wanted you to behave normally, as you had befriended the couple," Meecham explained. "We didn't want you to reveal, involuntarily, that you knew."

"Normal behavior in abnormal circumstances can prove a trifle hazardous," Esther pointed out.

Clifford resumed his explanation. "You will find, when you get home, Miss Lowden, that the pair of them cleared out their rooms. Had their things smuggled into his carriage and taken to London, pretending the carriage needed repairs. They had no intention of even paying their shot at your inn, but if you submit your bill, I'll see it's paid from his funds. He has plenty of them here and there. He'd planned to leave his white mount behind. A small price to pay for what he might have gotten away with this night."

Esther nodded. "He has a gold locket of mine I'd like to recover. It belonged to my mother. I still don't know who was sleeping in my attic. That wouldn't have been Fletcher, when he had his own suite and Cathy hers."

"Surely it was him, throwing a few red herrings in our path. He never slept a wink there, but only made up a mattress and tossed a few wine bottles about to make us think it was some outsider. And the cigar butt, as he don't smoke. He'd have picked it up around the hotel somewhere. He's full of twists, that one. He stuffs his lanky shoulders with wadding when he goes out robbing, to make his victims think he's a big lad, and of course the cape and hat add a touch of drama."

"I wonder where he got the capes and hats tonight."

"I was keeping an eye on him," Meecham said. "I noticed he and the woman went outside, and after they went back in, I had a look around. Two capes and hats were hidden in the shrubbery. The pistols must have been wrapped up in the capes. I daresay their man from the boat—Fletcher's groom cum valet—smuggled those items up to the Abbey."

Esther was aware that Meecham's laughing eyes were often trained on her as they talked. "I'm sorry I accused you, Mr. Meecham," she said. "Your timely arrival at the inn and rather suspicious behaviour led me astray."

"I told you why I went creeping into Fletcher's room—to see if he was there."

"I heard you were making inquiries in the taproom when you first arrived, and suddenly you and Joshua were old friends." Esther prodded.

"Our friendship is much older, actually. Josh and I discussed my coming in London. He's been trying to capture Captain Johnnie for a year now. I have no official capacity, but he thought a pair of ears at the inn might be helpful, and of course another rider with him on the heath at night. He thought my army experience might be useful. It was a venture after my own heart. As an old army type, I miss the excitement of the chase. Josh thought his importing an officer might alert Johnnie to what he was up to, so we decided we were new friends."

Esther looked at Joshua, no longer surprised that this stalwart gentleman was accustomed to taking to the heath. "Don't ask why I didn't tell you," Josh said. "You spent half your time in Fletcher's pocket.

We didn't want you dropping any hints. Paul was posing as a connection of mine to account for our necessarily being together, but we didn't want it known that I had sent for him specifically to trap the highwayman. In fact, I would have preferred it if his army past could remain unknown as well, but you soon ferreted out that secret, Esther, and rather than raise a mystery, we decided to admit to it."

Esther decided not to take offense and turned again to Meecham. "I did wonder, you know, when I saw you down at my old abandoned barn and learned of your secret tours of the attic and cellars."

"I was merely trying to see what use Johnnie planned to put them to. The evidence suggests he used the barn for some of his early work. I think the wine, however, was not stolen from your inn, but from the Black Knight. Clifford checked it for us, and they use the same sort. Once you set a guard on your stable, he had to abandon it and had mounts forwarded from the Black Knight. Half the horseflesh in the stable there is his. Your cellar was no good, as it had no outside door, and Buck was so often in his office, guarding the secret passage."

"He seemed more interested in the attics. I recall he asked several questions about whether I planned to use them during the coming boxing match. Why did you go to the heath when I set my poor trap?" Esther asked. "Surely you didn't think such an obvious trick would trap the Scamp?"

"It was his trip to London—that is, to the Black Knight to meet his 'sister,'—that decided us he might tackle your imaginary Wrothams that night. It was worth a try at least," Meecham explained.

"And why did you barricade your room door

211

against me?—doing considerable damage to the door frame, I might add."

"Not against you! Against the Scamp. My room was searched the day after I arrived."

"That was Buck!" Esther said, and turned pink at the admission.

Meecham ignored it, like a gentleman, and continued. "I had a few bits and pieces I didn't want him to see. Well, the cape and mask for one thing. Josh and I wore them when we went patrolling the heath. Josh is such a modest fellow, he didn't want his neighbors recognizing him."

"Yes, indeed," Esther agreed ironically. "He is so modest, he didn't even want you to know the masquerade party was in your honor, Mr. Meecham, and let on it was for me."

"When Mr. Clifford found those items suspicious, we came up with the idea of a masquerade ball," he said.

"I still found it suspicious," Clifford exclaimed.

"Yes, and that is why we finally had to take you into our confidence," Josh explained. "We would have done so sooner, but I know the runners' view on civilian interference. You would have forbidden us to ride out after Johnnie on our own."

"There's one thing I still want to discover from you, Meecham," Esther said. "Why did you enter your room by a ladder the first night you were at the inn? That is what initially set you up as a suspect."

"And it was designed to do just the opposite." Meecham laughed. "Josh rode out to meet me as I came from London. We saw the Higginses straggling toward town and assumed they had fallen victim to Johnnie. I mentioned to Josh that if I landed in at the inn two steps behind them, I might be suspected. I was a newcomer to town and rode a dark mount. I had left the inn at a time that made me the possible perpetrator. Josh suggested I slip in the window and pretend I had been in my room for some time. I do like the fresh air and leave my window open when I'm a safe distance from the ground. The ladder was there. . . ."

"And you hadn't yet discovered the trick of using the quoins as stairs." Esther smiled.

"True, I only learned that after I knew it was ineligible to leave a rope hanging. It wouldn't normally be seen at night, but with the sharp-eyed Miss Lowdon on guard, it was unwise."

Clifford rose and stretched his arms. "Any further details can wait till morning. I don't know about the rest of you, but this old carcass is for the feather tick."

"This one as well," Meecham added, and they left together.

Esther sighed and said to Joshua, "This aging parcel of flesh and bones is about ready for bed as well. Shall we go, Josh?"

He looked surprised. "Why it's only—"

"Only twenty to five, practically sunrise."

"We haven't had time to talk."

Esther yawned into her fist. "No time to talk? We've been talking for hours."

"But not about us." He rose from his chair and sat beside her on the sofa. "Only about your other beau, Captain Johnnie. I hope this convinces you that you would be better off with a man you've known longer.

Esther gave him a teasing look. "Buck, do you mean? Or Meecham?" She felt this Joshua who had suddenly turned heroic was half a stranger.

"Buck will be busy running the inn. Meecham, I

hope, will marry Margaret and buy the Pilchener house from me. He really is interested in settling here. I made an offer on Pilchener's estate."

"I know."

He looked a question. She continued, "You're not the only one who was trying to catch Johnnie. Where is Meecham going to get money to buy the house?"

"Lady Margaret's dot is generous enough to permit it—if she'll have him. I rather think she will. She wants to marry, and Paul is a good fellow. It would lighten my mortgage payments somewhat. I invited her here on this occasion hoping the two would be attracted. I believe my simple stratagem worked. We'll be a little pinched for a while with mortgage payments, but it will be worth it. Between Pilchener's place, the Abbey, and our inn, we'll be the largest landowners in the county."

Esther, like any clever lady, honed in on the most significant word in his speech. "*Our* inn, Josh?"

"To be precise, the inn belonging to the Lowden Investment Company. I don't think we should sell it after all, if it's making three thousand per annum."

"I'm only Queen of the May, not a royal highness! When did *I* become *we*?"

He reached for her fingers and squeezed them. "It has been a slow transformation. I believe the final fusion occurred when I saw Johnnie holding that gun to your back. I knew that if anything happened to you, it would be as if a part of myself died, too. Why did you do it?" His voice rose in frustration, but he quickly damped it back down to ardor. "I shouldn't ask. I can understand the allure of danger well enough."

Esther waited, and when he said no more, she

said, "Perhaps if you could let off arguing about my calling—"

"I have no objection to your being the mistress of Heath Abbey. That is the calling I have in mind."

She waited. There was passion in his eyes and voice, but it had not yet extended to other parts of his body. "I see," she said unhelpfully.

Joshua studied her for acceptance. "I know you have a fancy for more romantic gentlemen. I daresay I seem a dull old farmer to you, but now that you've had a taste of the other side of Captain Johnnie—"

A dreamy look possessed her. It was the other side of Joshua that caused it—that dashing side that enjoyed donning a mask and cape and riding into the dark danger of the heath. But when she answered, she said, "I wonder who my Captain Johnnie was, the one who kissed me on the heath."

"Kissed you! You didn't tell me that!"

"Did I not? It happened when I was with Beau and Cathy. Some friend of his, I am convinced. Probably a footman from the Black Knight."

"And you let him!"

"How could I stop a full-grown man?" she said innocently.

Joshua took the hint and pulled her into his arms for a satisfyingly violent kiss that raised a memory of that kiss on the heath. Behind closed eyes she imagined the starry sky. The strong arms crushing her were not the arms of a farmer but a demanding lover. His passion was hot and grew more fevered as she returned the pressure of his embrace. There was a romantic hiding in Joshua, as there was a dullard in the real Captain Johnnie, who could be satisfied with the simpleminded, irritating Cathy Barker for his lover. Esther encouraged the Scamp in Joshua, till propriety and fatigue brought it to a halt.

"We'll discuss this further tomorrow," she said primly.

Josh grazed a finger possessively along her cheek, while his dark eyes smiled lazily into hers. "It will take a deal of discussion, but the important matter is settled, Mrs. Ramsay. You and your aunt can discuss gowns and dates and menus, but do it quickly. I want my wife here, where I can keep an eye on her."

Then he closed his eyes and kissed her again.

14